INNOCENT SALVATION

SHADOW ELITE BOOK TWO

MADDIE WADE

Innocent Salvation
Shadow Elite Book Two
By Maddie Wade

Published by Maddie Wade
Copyright © February 2022

Cover: Clem Parsons-Metatec
Editing: Black Opal Editing
Formatting: Black Opal Editing

ACKNOWLEDGMENTS

I am so lucky to have such an amazing team around me without which I could never bring my books to life. I am so grateful to have you in my life, you are more than friends you are so essential to my life.

My wonderful beta team, Greta, and Deanna who are brutally honest and beautifully kind. If it is rubbish you tell me, it is and if you love it you are effusive. Your support means so much to me.

My editor—Linda at Black Opal Editing, who is so patient. She is so much more than an editor she is a teacher and friend.

Thank you to my group Maddie's Minxes. Your support and love for Fortis, Eidolon, Ryoshi and now Shadow Elite. You are so important to me. Special thanks to Rowena, Tracey, Faith, Rachel, Carolyn, Kellie, Maria, Rochelle, Becky, Vicky, Greta, Deanna, Sharon and Linda L for making the group such a friendly place to be.

My UK PA Clem Parsons who listens to all my ramblings and helps me every single day.

My ARC Team for not keeping me on edge too long while I wait for feedback.

Lastly and most importantly thank you to my readers who have embraced my books so wholeheartedly and shown a love for the stories in my head. To hear you say that you see my characters as family makes me so humble and proud. I hope you enjoy Snow and Sebastian's love story as much as I did.

Cover: Clem Parsons @Metatec
Editing: Black Opal Editing
Model: Rhylan Streloff

To all those women struggling with menopause. I see you.

PROLOGUE

HOLDING HER BREATH, SNOW TRIED TO STOP THE PANIC THAT ROSE IN HER throat, the memories hitting her, as a wave of grief cut through her belly like a scythe. Now wasn't the time to relive that night, not when she was about to pull off the biggest job of her life so far. Yet even knowing what she was about to do didn't give her the same rush as it had. Nothing was the same without him, and she'd have to live the rest of her life with that hollow ache in her chest.

What she could do was make him proud. Henri Goubert had been the best jewel thief in the world and had taught her everything he knew. From the moment she could walk he'd been training her.

Closing her eyes, she focused on the task at hand, which was lowering her body from the ventilation duct down to the main floor without tripping any of the laser alarms that crisscrossed the floor. The nickname had been given to her by her father because of her white-blonde hair he'd said looked like fresh snow.

Loosening the rope, she lowered herself slowly, each painful centimetre making the sweat bead on her brow, the mask over her head catching the droplets before they could set off the alarms and give the game away.

That's what this had always been to her—a game of wits and wills to see who was better. It was how her father made it seem to her as a child but as she grew up and became an adult, she knew what they did was wrong. Henri had always insisted it was a victimless crime and that made it okay.

Her father had never killed anyone or harmed a single person in his life, and she respected him for that. Snow had never had a thirst for blood either, until that day six years ago when her world had been turned on its head and everything she knew had been thrown into question. Now death was on her mind all the time and this job would give her the finances she'd need to fund her campaign of terror against the person who'd taken everything she loved from her.

Lifting her leg, she arched it over her head and balanced like the finest ballerina on her toe as her foot hit the ground. Now all she needed to do was get to the panel and disable the alarm and she was almost home free. Being supple was a gift in this game, and her father had always said in another life she could've been a ballerina but that wasn't her life and never would be, no matter how much she craved the freedom of it.

Sliding along the floor, taking care not to lift too high and set the laser off, Snow came to a stop beside the panel. Taking out her kit from her leg pocket she unscrewed the fixers and used the key she'd stolen to stop the alarm on the panel from erupting and alerting the whole of Rome—a place she'd spent a lot of time and loved.

The beauty, the food, the people, the places, and the ability to just get lost in the myriad of life going on around her. Also, the place with the biggest fine jewellers in all of Europe.

The alarm took longer than she expected but after a few minutes the light blinked out and she let out a small breath of relief. Now to get her haul and get out of there before she was caught. Jose had promised her he already had a buyer for this and once the sale was complete, she could get out of Rome and move on to London.

Walking across the main floor she took in the priceless jewels, diamonds, emeralds, and rubies, all twinkling, and wondered what it would be like to be a woman who wore them rather than one who stole them. Oh, she'd briefly felt the weight of a diamond necklace at her throat but only when she was in disguise as a guest at a function she and her father were robbing.

Dismissing the melancholy that had assailed her, she moved past the cases of jewels and headed for the back room where she knew the safe held the rarest of pink diamonds—the Rose Blossom. It would net her a cool six million dollars and was estimated to be worth almost fifty-eight million dollars. She didn't feel bad, these people were insured and by taking only what she'd come for she was exposing a weakness in their security.

She slid off her black glove and using the latex fingerprint opened the first locked door. Putting her glove back on she moved to the next room, which held the final hurdle of the night yet was surprisingly the easiest to obtain. It was funny what men would do for a kiss or touch, what secrets they'd tell, and getting the code for this door was incredibly easy.

The manager had even bragged he could put the code on his social media, and it wouldn't matter because nobody would get past his security system. Oh, wouldn't he feel foolish in the morning, but it was a valuable lesson to never trust anyone, no matter how innocent they might look.

The lock clicked, and she slowly opened the safe, revealing the Rose Blossom in all its glory on a bed of black velvet. Snow closed her eyes for a second, taking in the scent of everything in the room, and the hair on the back of her neck stood up as she registered a scent that shouldn't be there.

Clenching her fist, she palmed the knife she carried for protection, wishing she'd ignored her father and brought a gun. She was certainly competent with one now after six years of training day and night to fend off the nightmares of watching her father as he lay dying.

Luckily her hand-to-hand combat was good, more than good. Her body was her best weapon and, as agile and fit as she was, it worked in her favour, as well as her tiny size of barely five foot and half an inch, that half inch being very pertinent when you were so petite.

Sensing the stillness behind her, she tried to figure out where the threat was coming from but couldn't place it. It was as if he or she was a ghost and, as she spun around and found nobody there, she wondered if it was indeed the spirit of her dead father watching over her.

Checking the room with a quick glance, Snow turned back to the safe, deciding it was time to get the hell out before her paranoia got the better of her. Tucking the diamond into her belt, she pushed the safe closed and walked out of the room, only to stop short when a man dressed in black stepped in front of her.

She couldn't see his face as it was covered, as was hers, but she knew a predator when she was in the presence of one and he was the biggest predator she'd ever met. Lashing out with the blade in front of her she moved sideways. "I don't want to hurt you, but I will if I have to. Just let me leave and forget this night happened."

The man who had to be way over six feet cocked his head as if in thought. He was big, muscular, and moved with a smoothness she'd only ever seen once before.

"I'm afraid I can't do that, Snow."

Her body locked up at the British accent saying her name. Fear ran down her spine, making her body tingle. Not wanting him to see how affected she was, she controlled her reaction. "You have me at a disadvantage. You know who I am, but I don't know you."

"All you need to know for now is that your father sent me."

Pain was like a lance through her chest at the cruelty of the man insinuating her father could have sent him. "My father is dead."

He cocked his head as if assessing the information before he spoke. "I know and I'm sorry for that, but I was sent in the event of his death. I'm here to help."

"I don't need your help."

As if on cue, the man cocked his head again and the sounds of police sirens hit her ears.

"That's the police, and they're coming here to catch you. The man who gave you the code to the safe works for Interpol, and as you know, they've been wanting to catch you for years now."

Snow felt panic and anger at herself for being so damn arrogant fill her throat with bile. "Time for me to leave then."

Snow went to push past the man sensing he wouldn't hurt her and as he stepped aside, she knew she'd been right.

"Snow, I'm offering you a place within my organisation, to live free, to work for me doing what you do best but without the risk of being caught."

Snow rounded on him. "Why?"

"Because we have need of someone with your skills and because your father, although not a good man, wasn't a bad one. He loved you and wanted more for you than this life."

"Why should I trust you?"

"You shouldn't. You should trust your gut and you know I'm not here to hurt you. If I was, we both know I would've killed you by now."

She knew that was the truth. Reading people was one of her many talents, part learned, part instinct. When you people watched as much as she did it was easy to see the tells. Her gut was telling her she could trust this man. "I can't. I have a mission of my own and I mean to finish solo."

"Let us help you, Snow. If you go after Dominique now, you'll fail, and any chance at retribution will be gone. Play the long game and I'll make sure you get your chance to avenge your father and find your niece."

The sounds of sirens were louder now, and she knew she had less than two minutes to get away before she was carted off in handcuffs, yet she couldn't walk away from what he'd just said. "Niece?"

She had no knowledge of a niece. Oh, she knew of her sibling, even if he'd never know about her, nor would she wish him to. He was as toxic as the woman who'd spawned him, but a child was innocent, and she wouldn't leave an innocent child subjected to that kind of evil.

The man held his hand out. "Come with me."

She paused, trying to make the right choice, and wishing for the thousandth time her father was there to guide her. "Fine."

"Put the diamond back first. You won't need it."

Snow baulked but the man didn't flinch, and she wondered again just who the hell he was.

Time had run out as the cars screeched to a halt outside, so she reluctantly put the diamond back and followed the man who led her through the back, seemingly talking to someone on comms as he led her into the back alley that ran the length of the street. They ran, rounding a corner until a car drew up, the door flying open as he ushered her inside.

Snow had no idea who these people were, but it was clear they didn't want to hurt her, and had, in fact, just saved her from spending the next twenty years in prison. As the car sped away the man pulled the mask from his face revealing a strong jaw and chin and deep blue eyes. Thick dark hair covered his head and although older than her, Snow appreciated that he was a handsome man.

Knowing he was trusting her with his identity, she felt compelled to do the same and slowly removed her own covering.

A twitch of approval at the man's lips made her wonder if he'd expected her to hide, but that had never been her personality. Although the person she was now wasn't the same as before. Watching her father murdered in cold blood had sapped her natural happiness.

"So now what?"

"Now we get you out of Rome."

"And then?" Was she seriously considering this madness with people she didn't know?

"Then, we train you and we turn you into an asset."

"What about my niece and my revenge?"

6

"We'll help you, but you need to be smart. Running in this way will get you killed. If you want to bring down your enemy, then as I said, you play the long game. For now, your niece is safe and well taken care of by her mother and uncle."

"How did you know my father?"

The man smiled as if remembering a fond memory. "Let's just say your father and I had a few run-ins and eventually came to an understanding."

"He robbed you?"

"No, he tried to steal from my employer, and I couldn't allow that, but he also agreed to become an informant in exchange for me looking the other way on certain things."

"My dad was a confidential informant?"

"In a manner of speaking yes, but I'm not the police."

Snow eyed him and then the back of the head of the man who drove them, his brown eyes meeting hers in the mirror. "And he sent you to help me in the event of his death?"

"Yes."

"How do I know you aren't lying."

"You don't, but how else would I know you have a scar on your thumb from trying to squash a hornet, which you thought was a wasp when you were eight. That you have a knife wound on your shoulder blade from a close encounter with a security guard in a Polish private residence. Or that your mother is Dominique Dupont and that she handed you over to your father and asked him to end your life because she couldn't afford the scandal."

Snow gasped, her hand flying to her mouth knowing that nobody on this earth except her father had that painful knowledge. Nobody wanted to feel unloved, and while she hated her mother with a passion as white-hot as the sun, it still shamed her that she wanted her dead and that was why nobody but she and her father knew that. He'd only told her because he never wanted to risk her trusting the viper, as he'd called her, and falling into any trap she might set. Henri Goubert had been a wonderful father and not once had she questioned his love and loyalty to her. Even now he was protecting her and showing her a way out of the spiral of revenge that was taking over her life.

"Okay."

Snow stuck out her hand for the man, a smile on her face that felt like the first real emotion she'd felt in a long time. He took her small palm in his and gave it a firm shake.

"Sabine Goubert, I'm Jack Granger and I'd like you to join Shadow Elite."

"Then I accept your offer. Although we need to discuss salary, benefits, holiday pay, sick pay, etcetera etcetera."

Jack threw his head back and laughed. "You're going to be a breath of fresh air for the team."

Snow hoped so because she was tired of being alone.

CHAPTER I

"Snow, what can I do for you?"

Snow placed the printout she'd been looking at for the last two hours on Bás' desk.

He picked it up and read the names on the list before his head raised to look at her. "What is this?"

"Watchdog found it in Doyle's files."

Bás leaned back in his chair regarding her as she tried not to fidget and show how much she had invested in this. "And?"

"You know who those people are?"

Bás snorted and picked up the paper again. "Dominique Dupont and Sebastian Alexander." He looked at her again and motioned for her to sit, which she did. "Tell me what's going on with you, Snow, and don't fucking lie to me."

Snow considered lying. She needed this job and Bás would go ballistic if he found out she was keeping secrets. It was the one thing he wouldn't tolerate. "I want to know what Dominique and Judge Alexander are involved with."

Bás showed no emotion at all when she said the woman's name

and she wondered if he already knew her background and guessed it was a possibility. "Why now? What caused this sudden interest?"

Snow produced a picture of a little girl no more than four years old, her sweet face smiling at the camera. Her heart clenched with pain, and she had to hold a hand to her belly to steady herself. Pushing the image toward Bás, she swallowed the bile in her throat. "Because that's my niece that Judge Alexander is raising, and I want to know why."

Snow thought Bás would react but still nothing, and it was frustrating.

"How is this Shadow business?"

Snow clenched her fist and released it, hoping she could remain calm. Her personality was bright and cheery, but she had a quick temper that got her into trouble. "Judge Alexander is leading the inquiry into the corruption trial against the men who helped Doyle. If he's dirty, then it's our business."

"Is it just Alexander you're interested in or Dominique too?"

Just her name made Snow see red. The woman swanned around like she shit roses, making speeches and acting as if she were the epitome of perfection and truth, and yet she was the dirtiest of them all. "She's as dirty as hell, and you know it as well as I do."

"I do know that but going after her isn't something we'd do lightly. A woman like her will have her skeletons well hidden. She won't take risks with her reputation, and you can bet your ass she has people to deal with these things for her."

"Oh, I know that better than most but there's one skeleton she can't walk away from, and I can prove it."

"Oh?"

"She murdered my father."

Bás raised his one brow for her to keep going. "How do you know this?"

"Because I watched her do it when I was sixteen years old." Snow waved her hand in the air. "She didn't actually fire the gun, but she stood and watched as her men tortured and killed him."

"Why would she want him dead?"

"Because he held the key to her weakness."

"And that is?"

"Me! I'm the key because I'm the daughter she gave away like rubbish and told my father to dispose of. I'm the daughter of the President of France and it's time she paid for her crimes." She was breathing hard, the pain of reliving the worst day of her life taking its toll on her nerves.

"I take it if you're here you have a plan?"

Snow tried not to show her excitement but failed as she leaned forward. "Alexander needs a nanny for the girl. I can get in and find the proof we need of any involvement or corruption and check on my niece at the same time."

"You really think getting up close and personal is a good idea? Duchess and Lotus normally handle the undercover work?"

"No, this is mine. I can do this, Bás."

"Judge Alexander won't be a pushover. He's the youngest court of appeals judge in history at thirty-five and has the money behind him to back up his power. He's old money and has a reputation as a hardass. You sure you can handle that? He's the antithesis to your sunny disposition."

"I'm there for the kid. You just need to make sure I get an interview and I can do the rest."

"Fine, but you don't go alone. I want Reaper to go with you. Use the flat in Kensington and pretend he's your roommate."

"Fine."

"I'll call a meeting and inform the others of the plan." Bás linked his fingers and leaned forward. "But if I think for one second you've lost control or gone off-book, I'll pull you out faster than you can blink."

"I won't let you down, Bás."

"It's not me I'm worried about."

Snow walked from the room and headed back to her quarters. Going to her desk she took out the image of Sebastian Alexander. He was a handsome devil. He had dark hair with a slight curl that was barely contained, tanned skin, a strong jaw, and he filled a suit in a way that male models would hang themselves from the rafters for.

It didn't matter though, because she'd never be attracted to a man who could smile at Dominique like he was in this picture. No, a man like that would never have her heart or her body. He was the enemy, and she was going to destroy him.

CHAPTER 2

"All rise for the honourable Judge Alexander."

Sebastian strode through from the side door and up onto the podium to his bench. He dropped a slight bow to the court and then sat. "Be seated."

Sebastian motioned for the clerk to read the case so they could begin. He knew the case of course. He made sure he knew every finite detail of a case he was presiding over so that nothing would get past him. He'd worked his ass off to get to this prestigious position and he knew there were still those in the House of Lords who thought he was too young for the job. So, he'd just keep proving to them how good he was until it wasn't in question any longer.

He glanced down at his notes as the defence lawyer began his opening statements. This was the case of a serial rapist who'd gone free for five years before finally being caught after his last victim was killed. His job was to remain impartial, to make sure the case he presided over was fair and just and guide the court so that it remained that way.

Three hours in and he could see the jury were beginning to wane. A case like this was difficult for the most hardened of officials, hearing the testimony and seeing the images of the crimes could be exhausting, and it was also his role to make sure the jury got enough breaks to be able to see the case clearly.

The fact this man had pled not guilty to the crimes meant that every piece of evidence would be taken out, examined, argued over, and discredited. That took time, and while he always tried his absolute best to remain impartial, he always had a sense of whether the defendant was guilty. It was what had made him such a good barrister. This man in front of him in the dock was as guilty as sin, but despite his title his job wasn't to judge, it was to guide.

"Let's take a break for one hour and court will restart at fourteen-thirty."

Sebastian stood gave a short bow and headed for his office. He passed his secretary on the way who was heading towards him with a stack of messages and paperwork.

"Your lunch is on your desk, Judge."

"Thank you, Margaret."

Margaret had been with him for five years and knew all his habits and quirks. She was in her late fifties, although he wasn't entirely sure of her age, and had two grown sons who ran their own architectural firm.

"Here are your messages."

Margaret knew he didn't like his messages being called out to him like he was a child who couldn't read, so she always left them on his desk to read. For a judge, he wasn't a people person, or perhaps because of it. He'd seen the very worst of humankind and from his experience, especially of late, less and less of the kindness.

His chest ached as he thought of Lucinda, at the loss of someone with so much spirit, so much heart, and the world to live for. He'd never forgive himself for not seeing her pain, for not being aware of just how ill she was. He'd failed her the same way their parents had, and he'd take that guilt to the grave.

The only thing he could do now was make it up to her daughter, the niece he was trying to raise with no clue how to do it. If people were an enigma to him, children were the equivalent of aliens, and his four-year-old niece Fleur was the queen of them.

He picked up the picture on his desk of his sister and niece from last Christmas when they'd gone skiing in France and smiled. His money and wealth allowed him to give the few people he cared for everything he could. Lucinda had never been about the money they'd inherited from the family holdings and business ventures. She'd been a free spirit, more at home in her long, flowy skirts painting in the meadow with the sun on her face.

Now all that was gone, and he was left to pick up the pieces after the man who was meant to love her broke her in a way she could never heal from.

Bitterness and hate twisted in his gut for the weak, pathetic man who swanned around after his famous parent, sucking up all the praise and acclaim he could leech from her. He was nothing but a parasite and so was the witch who'd spawned him. They'd never get their filthy hands on Fleur though, if it was the last thing he did. He'd break every oath and law he'd ever uttered to keep that little girl safe.

Picking up the phone, he dialled his home and waited for it to pick up.

"Alexander residence."

"It's me. Put Fleur on the phone."

Sebastian never wasted time on pleasantries. They were his staff, not his friends, and he paid them all a hefty salary to do the job. He had two people he considered friends, and they were Judd Lafferty and Oliver Jones, his roommates from Eton and his best friends. They'd been there for him at every milestone event in his life and he trusted them and only them.

"Uncy Seb."

An involuntary smile tugged at his lips at the sound of her butchering the word uncle. "Hello, Fleur, how are you today?"

"I bored. Miss Moss is making me do letters again."

The way she dragged out the words as if this was the height of torture made him smile. He was determined she'd get the best education money could buy. "But letters are good. They make all the fun words you like to say."

"Like what?"

"Spaghetti."

"I like sgabetti. Can we have sgabetti for dinner tonight?"

"Ask Mrs Lewis if she'll make it for you. I might be late tonight."

"But you promised we'd have a tea party."

Damn it, he had too. He hated to let her down, but the judiciary process wasn't likely to accept a child's tea party as a reason to end the day early unless it fell at a crucial point.

"I'm sorry, Fleur, but I'll make it up to you. How about we go to the Zoo this weekend?"

"You promise?"

"On my honour."

The phone clattered and he could hear her running toward Mrs Lewis, who was his housekeeper and had been since his parents were alive, yelling in excitement about elephants.

Sebastian smiled to himself once more and hung up the phone. That little girl was the most important person in his life, and he loved her and would protect her from everyone and anything in a way he hadn't managed with his sister.

Noticing he had very little time left, Sebastian wolfed his lunch of turkey salad on wholegrain bread down, taking care not to get it on his robes. He read his messages deciding which were important and which could wait and made a note for Margaret.

Taking a sip of water, he went to wash his hands and had just straightened his robes when a knock sounded on the door. "Enter."

The click of heels indicated exactly who it was, and he sighed impatiently. He didn't have the time or inclination to deal with this right now, although he was surprised it took this long for her to seek him out.

"Judge Alexander."

His name was a purr on her red lips as he stepped out into his office drying his hands and saw Julianne Talbot standing by his desk.

Julianne was beautiful, tall, with long dark hair which was currently secured in a neat bun at the back of her head. A slim yet curvy figure and dark chestnut-coloured eyes. She was the prosecution lawyer for this case and someone he'd fucked a few times.

A mistake he wouldn't be making again. She was ambitious and cunning, sucked cock like it was her job, and until recently had been happy to keep things simple and uncomplicated by unnecessary emotions, but the last time he'd left her bed, she'd complained about him leaving to go home to Fleur and whined about his lack of attention. Little did she know that had sealed her fate, and whatever arrangement they'd had was now over.

"Julianne, what can I do for you?"

She stalked closer and he wondered if she made other men feel like prey. Her hand skimmed down his arm and he took a subtle step back so she was no longer touching him. Her pout, so attractive before, merely aggravated him now and made her look ridiculous.

"I've missed you these last few weeks. I thought maybe we could catch up this weekend and spend some time getting reacquainted."

"No, I'm busy this weekend with Fleur."

He caught the way her eyes tightened in annoyance and knew he'd done the right thing. While he wasn't looking for a wife or girl-friend, any woman he spent time with had to at least understand that Fleur came first and would always come first. This woman was a great lawyer, but she had all the maternal instincts of a snake.

"What about next weekend?"

"No, let me make this clear for you, Julianne. We had fun but now that it's over, none of my free time will be available to you. Is that clear?"

He saw her pale before going bright red, not with upset, but from anger and humiliation. Perhaps he should have been kinder, but he'd learned that with a woman like this it was best to be clear.

"So, we fucked and now you want to throw me away like trash?"

"We fucked and had fun and now it's over."

"So, you used me?"

Her breathing was coming faster the angrier she got and, once upon a time, he would've found her heaving tits a turn on but now he found it an irritation. He had no desire to be there with her. "I think we used each other."

"Oh no, Judge, you used me. You're the one in the position of power here."

His body went still, his jaw clenching as anger infused his body that she was daring to threaten him that way when she'd been the instigator in their affair.

He moved a step closer but kept his hands by his sides and, with his voice low and deep, spoke words he'd hoped to never utter. "Julianne, if you ever threaten me again, I'll end you. We both know very well that you made the first move in this very office, and if you remember you signed an NDA and it's stated in it that you made the first move. Now, you're a good lawyer with a great career in front of you. I suggest you concentrate on that and stay the hell away from me because if we have to have this conversation again, it won't be a friendly warning."

Sebastian stepped back behind his desk putting space between them so he didn't wring her scrawny neck and busied himself with his papers. He heard a huff before she turned on her heel and strode out of the room. Lifting his phone, he dialled Margaret.

"Yes, Judge?"

"Don't let that woman into my office again without an appointment or checking with me first."

"Yes, Judge."

Sebastian hung up and placed the wig he wore into court back on his head. It itched like hell in the summer, but it was all part of the performance, and he'd play his part to perfection.

Ten minutes later he was about to walk into court when the clerk informed him that the prosecuting counsel had gone home sick and could they postpone until tomorrow. Relieved his day was over he agreed and was soon driving his green jaguar through the London traffic towards Mayfair where he lived.

Grabbing his jacket and briefcase, he took the steps two at a time and pushed through the door. He placed his suit jacket on the entry table and loosened his tie as the sound of shouting and a crying child hit his ears.

Prowling quickly through the hallway, he made his way toward the sound and stopped in shock and outrage at the scene before him. Ms Moss, the nanny, had hold of Fleur and was dragging her towards the small desk he'd set up for her to use in the nursery room that had been converted from the conservatory.

"You little brat, you'll learn some manners."

Before he knew what he was doing, he was across the room, flinging the shocked woman's hand away from a crying Fleur and gathering the child into his arms.

"Mr Alexander, I wasn't expecting you."

He was so furious he could hardly see for the rage inside him. Never in his life had he been violent with a woman but in that second the only thing stopping him from doing her serious harm was the way Fleur curled into his body, her small arms tight around his neck, her breath tickling his neck as she whimpered. "That's very clear. Pack your things and get out of my house this second."

"But, Mr Alexander, I can explain."

His body was vibrating with rage as he stepped forward and something in his face must have made it clear he wasn't fucking around. "Nothing you can say will explain you putting your hands on my niece. Now get your fucking bags packed and get out. I'll be calling the agency as soon as I calm my niece and you'll never work in this industry again."

Ms Moss, who was probably fortyish, began to cry as she rushed past him to her rooms, which were situated in the converted attic space.

Carrying Fleur to the seat that was way too small for his huge frame, he sat down with her still clinging to him and tried to pry her from his neck. "Hey, munchkin, are you okay?"

Fleur sniffed and wiped her face on his five-hundred-pound shirt before she nodded.

"Want to tell me what happened?"

"Ms Moss said I was a bad girl because I didn't want to learn my letters and that I was just like my crazy mummy. I got mad 'cos Mummy was nice, and I didn't like her saying those things, so I kicked her bag over and she got really mad."

He wasn't sure he could get angrier after what he'd witnessed but it seemed he was wrong because in that instant he wanted to commit murder. How dare that woman be so cruel to a child. It was one of the reasons he avoided people; they truly sucked.

Brushing her blonde hair back from her wet cheeks, he kissed his niece's head and cuddled her close. "Your mummy was the best. She was good and kind and she loved you so much and anyone would be lucky to be like her. You shouldn't have kicked her bag over, but I'm proud of you for standing up for yourself. Don't ever let anyone push you around, and if they do, you tell me and I'll fix it for you, okay?"

"Okay, Uncy Seb."

"Good, now how about that tea party you promised me?"

"Really?"

"Yes, you set it up while I take out the rubbish and we can have cake and tea."

Fleur tightened her little arms around his neck, almost strangling him, she held on so tight.

"I love you, Uncy Seb."

His heart almost cracked open with the love he felt for this child, a love he knew deep down he'd never be able to give anyone else because he simply didn't have it in him to give and that was okay. She was all he needed now.

"I love you too, munchkin."

CHAPTER 3

HE'D DECIDED AFTER THE LAST FIASCO WITH MS MOSS THAT HE'D LET EACH potential nanny spend a few hours with Fleur under his watchful eye, or at least the watchful eye of a camera that he'd had Judd install. Judd owned a security tech company, which was now a huge success.

So far, he'd managed to find fault in all nine nannies the agency had sent over and today was his last chance before he had to find a new avenue to explore. He glanced down at the name of this one and rolled his eyes. Sabine Goubert, which instantly put his back up. She was obviously French and while he didn't hate the French, he had a certain wariness considering Fleur's absent and useless father was French, but maybe that would be in this woman's favour. She spoke the language and her CV was excellent with immaculate references. Perhaps a little younger than he would've liked at twenty-six but that wasn't a deal-breaker for him.

His phone buzzed in his home office, and he picked it up knowing it was internal. "Yes?"

"Breakfast is served, and Miss Fleur is asking for you."

"Tell her I'll be right down."

He made a point to always have breakfast with his niece when he was in town and not away on business. He knew it was important for them to spend at least one meal a day as a family. He didn't want her to grow up feeling like she didn't have a family who loved her. It might just be the two of them, but they were enough. He didn't want her feeling like a burden or an afterthought.

Tidying his desk, he exited the room and locked the door, as was his habit now after finding the four-year-old had drawn a stick man on a legal document he'd left on his desk in the first few weeks of them living together.

It had been a very steep learning curve for the both of them and he wasn't sure by any means they'd survived it yet, but they were getting there, slowly. The life he'd led as an eligible bachelor who could stay out all night drinking and fucking any woman he chose were gone. Now he had responsibilities he'd never seen coming and he'd give his last breath to turn back time. He couldn't so he'd do his best to love his niece enough for his sister and the useless asshole who'd sired her and never even held her.

Fleur's eyes lit up as he appeared and sat down to breakfast opposite her in the formal dining room. "Look, Uncy Seb, I have a face on my pancakes."

He looked to see the chocolate chips were in the pattern of a smiley face. "So you do."

He whipped the white napkin across his lap and began to eat his eggs and toast. Fleur filled the silence, not letting him get a word in as she ate, and he knew he should be stricter about her talking at breakfast as his parents had been, but he loved the sound of her chatter. His home had been so quiet and dead, now it was filled with life.

The doorbell rang and he glanced at the clock. The new nanny candidate wasn't due until nine am and it was only eight-forty-five. Standing, he went to the entranceway to see Mrs Lewis letting someone inside. He couldn't see from where he was what she looked like, so moved forward as Mrs Lewis stepped back.

He scowled at seeing her, and as his body tightened in unwanted lust at the sight of the woman, he knew she'd never work out. A woman who could evoke such a strong reaction in him wasn't a good person to have around.

She was petite, barely over five feet, with blonde hair that looked almost white and blue eyes that danced like ice diamonds. Pink lips full and ripe but slim build with just the hint of curves. She was nothing like his type and yet he wanted to strip her down in this hallway and find out if she tasted as sweet as she looked. If the twinkle in those eyes was as bright when she came from his touch. No, this wouldn't do.

"Ah, Mr Alexander, there you are. This is Ms Goubert, the new candidate for the nanny position." Mrs Lewis was smiling in encouragement, and it made the frown between his brows deepen.

He didn't know what to say. He was a powerful man, but words failed him as she stepped forward, her head barely reaching his shoulder and offered her hand. He took it and gave it a quick shake and a grunt of greeting before he pulled away, her touch sending electricity through his skin and up his arm. He wondered if she'd been affected but found he couldn't read her in the least, another thing he didn't like.

"It's very nice to meet you, Mr Alexander."

He detected a very slight accent in her voice and wondered how long she'd lived in the UK. Her voice was soft and had a happy, confidant quality to it which annoyed him because it instantly brought visions to mind of them laughing together. Steeling his features and emotions back under control, he locked his eyes on Ms Goubert.

He was about to send her away when her face lit up with a smile that took his breath away, and she crouched as Fleur came skidding past him to stop just in front of the woman. His hand shot out to stop Fleur from getting too close, his overprotective streak even more pronounced since the incident with Ms Moss.

"Hi, I'm Snow. What's your name?"

He glanced at Fleur who was wearing a similar expression to his own at the sound of the name she gave. His hand flexed lightly on the child's shoulder, and he smiled at her with reassurance when she looked at him for permission.

"I'm Fleur Louise Alexander and I am this big." Sebastian watched as Fleur held up four fingers indicating her age.

"Wow, that *is* big. You must be eating all your greens to get that big."

"Uncy Seb says that if you eat your greens you get to be big and strong."

Her eyes found his and again he couldn't read them. It annoyed the hell out of him, although he did detect warmth in them and a tiny twitch of her full lips.

"Well, your uncle is correct."

"Why are you called Snow? Snow isn't a name."

"Fleur." Sebastian agreed but he wouldn't have Fleur being rude to this woman even if her tenure would be short.

"It's fine, I get it a lot." Her eyes moved from him back to Fleur and he admired how she stayed focused on his niece at her eye level.

"Snow is a nickname, because of my hair. My friends say I can blend into the snow. My real name is Sabine."

Sebastian rolled that answer around in his head and found he liked the idea of her being compared to the purity of snow. He'd always liked the snow, the quiet, the peace, and the pure beauty of it.

"Uncy Seb, can I have a nickname?" Sebastian pulled his gaze away from the woman who was now watching him intently and focused on his niece.

"You already do. I call you munchkin."

He saw Fleur wrinkle her nose as if thinking and then patted his hand as if placating him. "It's okay, I'll think of one."

Sebastian tried not to smile at her trying to let him down gently. "You do that. Now, why don't you go in and finish your breakfast and let me speak with Ms Goubert for a moment?"

"Okay."

Fleur turned and waved at Snow before she skipped away. He watched, schooling his features into the mask of ice he wore in the courtroom before facing Ms Goubert again.

She was standing tall and she still only reached his chest.

"Thank you for coming, Ms Goubert, but I'm afraid this won't work out. I won't be needing your services."

Her blue eyes widened in surprise and disappointment and for a second, he felt the tiniest smidgen of guilt before he pushed it away. This was his home, and he couldn't have a woman he found this attractive in it with him and his niece. He needed to stay on track and give all his attention to Fleur.

"Oh! May I ask what it was that I did wrong?"

"Nothing, it just simply won't work. I need someone older, less..." He waved his hand at her trying to describe what he meant when he didn't know how to explain it himself.

"Less what?" Her short movement forward had him itching to step back away from the sweet scent of her perfume which was light and floral and reminded him of hot summer nights.

"Young."

"You do realise it's illegal to judge my ability based on my age?"

His jaw clenched in anger at being called out and his tone was flinty when he responded, his own body moving closer now to show his dominance. "I know the law, Ms Goubert."

"Then give me today to prove I'm good at this job and after that, if I'm not suitable, I'll happily walk away."

Sebastian cocked his head. Perhaps he'd underestimated this woman's backbone. She was beautiful to look at and had an aura of sweetness about her but inside he suspected after this was a backbone made of steel.

"And if I say no?" He hated being threatened and was prepared to throw this woman out on her sexy little ass if she tried.

"Then you're teaching your niece that hard work means nothing if your face doesn't fit. That as a woman you can be judged on your looks instead of your abilities."

Sebastian hadn't expected that or the wave of discomfort her words evoked. She'd called him out and she was right. If anyone treated his niece in this way he'd go berserk. "Fine, you have today to prove to me that you're suitable for this position. I'll be working from home today and if I get the slightest hint that you're not capable, you'll be out that door quicker than you can blink."

"I'd expect nothing less."

Sebastian pushed his hands into the pockets of his suit trousers before he turned with a short nod. "Follow me."

He set Fleur and Snow up in the playroom, which now had a camera linked to his laptop and gave her the schedule of things he expected Fleur to accomplish through the day.

She frowned as she read through it but said nothing, probably not wanting to give him a reason to get rid of her. Instead, he pushed, wanting her to fail so he could be away from her and the lust burning through his veins.

"This is great. We'll get right to it."

She turned and bestowed a radiant smile on Fleur before sinking to her knees beside his niece and ignoring him. Her action made him clench his teeth, every inappropriate thought he'd ever imagined flew into his head at her action and he wondered if she'd done it on purpose to try and tempt him. It wouldn't be the first time a woman had tried to seduce him by getting close to Fleur but when he glanced at her, she was facing away, her entire focus on his niece who was chattering away as if they were old friends.

Sebastian spent the day alternating between reading and re-reading case notes and watching Snow and Fleur on the camera. He wasn't sure if she was aware of the fact she was being watched but frustratingly she didn't put a foot wrong. She engaged Fleur in learning in a way that had the child begging to play the game again. She was firm but kind, somehow managed to get his niece to take a short nap after lunch and even made some improvements to the playroom with a number and letter chart.

Now he was in a predicament he hadn't seen coming. This woman was the best candidate for the position so far, more than exceeding his stringent requirements, and more importantly, Fleur liked her, and she seemed to like his niece. So, he needed to man up and give his niece what she needed. After all, she was what mattered most.

As he walked toward the playroom at the end of his unproductive workday, he knew what he had to do. "Ms Goubert, may I speak with you in private please?"

She handed Fleur a red crayon with a smile of encouragement and followed him out of the room.

He led her into the library and closed the door behind them before he turned to her, letting his gaze wander over her in a purely observant way. "You did well today. Despite my initial reservations, my niece likes you and you engaged with her well. I won't say I still don't have some misgivings, but I'm prepared to give you a chance and a trial period of one month."

Snow seemed to inflate, her smile widening, and she bounced on her toes like an excited puppy which he found rather annoying. "That's wonderful, I won't let you down, Mr Alexander."

"Good. See that you don't."

"May I ask what changed your mind?"

Sebastian didn't have to think about that, there was only one person who could change his mind about anything and that was Fleur. "My niece likes you and her opinion is important to me. In fact, it's the only opinion that I care about." He hoped he was making things clear to her but in case he was being too subtle he'd spell it out for her. "There are a few rules involved in your employment."

"All right."

"You have the rooms at the top of the house and your own bathroom, but you may use the kitchen when you need. No outside guests will be allowed into my home without my express permission and certainly no sleepovers. Your hours are seven in the morning to seven at night unless I need you to work late because I'm at work. Obviously, you can take breaks throughout the day when Fleur is asleep or resting. You may take weekends off, but I may ask you to work the odd occasion when I need to attend an event. You'll be given as much notice as I can possibly give you. You'll dress appropriately with no revealing clothing during work hours. What you do outside of that is your business as long as it doesn't impact myself or my niece in any way."

"That's all reasonable, although I'd like to ask what you mean by revealing clothes?"

His jaw twitched as he was made to explain what he meant when he couldn't quantify it. Shit, she was dressed in jeans and a pale blue flowered blouse that showed no skin and yet it still made his dick hard. "Nothing too low cut or skirts above mid-thigh."

"That's fine."

"One more thing. You're here to do a job, an important one. One that doesn't land you a rich husband so if you have any thoughts regarding that get them out of your head this second. I'm not looking for a hook up, fun, or benefits. I have my private life and certainly have zero interest in you. Is that clear?"

Now he got a reaction as her nostrils flared with what he could only assume was outrage. Her skin pinked at the cheeks, and he couldn't help but think how stunning she was angry.

"Perfectly, and for the record, I'm not looking for a sugar daddy. I make my own money and have no interest in you, Mr Alexander."

He'd offended her and he should feel bad but after the last few days it was difficult to see the wood for the trees and it was more important to be clear than to preserve her precious feelings. "Good, then we're all set. You can move in whenever you're ready and if you're available you can start first thing tomorrow."

"I can bring my stuff over tonight and will be ready for Fleur first thing in the morning."

"Good."

He pulled out a key and handed it to her. "Here's your key and I'll text you the alarm code."

He was careful not to let his fingers touch hers as he handed it over and yet he could still feel the pull between them. This may have been a mistake for him, but he felt sure it was the right thing for Fleur and she was the important one.

CHAPTER 4

PROMPTLY AT SEVEN AM THE NEXT MORNING, SNOW STEPPED INTO THE kitchen to see Mrs Lewis at the counter in the kitchen. The older woman turned and smiled warmly and pointed to the coffee pot.

"It's just brewed, my dear. Why don't you pour a cup before you head up to see Miss Fleur?"

Snow poured some of the fragrant rich coffee into the mug Mrs Lewis handed her and set it on the side after one sip.

"I best head up, don't want to get on the wrong side of the ogre on day one."

"He really isn't so bad when you get to know him a little, just reserved."

"I'll take your word for it."

Snow rushed out of the kitchen and ran slap bang into Sebastian Alexander who was lurking outside the kitchen. She felt her cheeks flame and wondered if he'd heard what she called him. Not that she cared really, he was an arrogant jerk who thought he was God's gift to women. She hated that she found him stupidly attractive and was relieved he was so unlikable, or she'd be in trouble.

His firm hands gripped her shoulders to steady her from landing on her bottom, releasing her as soon as he could.

"Are you okay, Ms Goubert?"

"Yes, just heading up to wake Fleur."

"No need. She's been awake for an hour already. You may need to help her with her outfit though."

"Oh, I thought you said I should start at seven."

"I did, but she's awake at five-thirty, and nobody should be made to work those kinds of hours, not even an ogre."

Snow flushed at his implication that he'd indeed heard every word. She wouldn't apologise though, this man was rude, conceited, and arrogant and he was an ogre with everyone. She just hoped he wasn't that way with her niece. "Well, I'll go help her."

Snow rushed off, feeling the heat of his gaze as she raced up the stairs. She found Fleur trying to stuff her legs into woolly tights of striped pink and orange and a yellow summer dress with stars on it. The outfit was nothing if not unique and she rolled her lips to hide her smile. She reminded her of herself at the same age, so sure, so independent.

"Need some help?"

"Snow, you came back."

"Yes of course I did. I had far too much fun yesterday to leave you."

Snow knelt beside Fleur and helped her pull the tights up to her waist before brushing the skirt flat. It was by no means a match, but it was important for Fleur to know she had a choice and could express herself however she saw fit.

Snow held out her hand. "Ready for breakfast?"

"Will you plait my hair first? Uncy Seb isn't good at it, but don't tell him I said so, it hurts his feelings and makes him sad."

Snow knew it was impossible to stop herself from falling in love with this child. She may not have time for the man who sired her or even know her mother, but she was blood and more than that, she was adorable. A rumble of protectiveness rushed over her, and she knew she'd do anything for this child. Even put up with her grump of an uncle.

"Yes, of course. Go grab me a hair band and brush and I'll see what I can do."

In no time she'd secured the child's hair in a braid down the back of her head and tied a bow at the end. Hand in hand they walked down the stairs and into the dining room where Mr Grump himself was seated at the head of the table like a king at a banquet.

"What would you like for breakfast, Fleur?"

"I want egg and toast soldiers and juice."

In unison, both she and Sebastian said, "Please."

Snow's eyes shot to his and him hers before she looked away and back to Fleur who was giggling.

"You just jinxed."

"We did, didn't we?"

"You have to do the thing."

Snow was standing beside Fleur on the opposite side to Sebastian who seemed to have no clue what she was talking about.

"I don't think your uncle knows about the thing, and he's far too busy."

"What thing?"

His voice was full of impatience and she glared at him as he frowned like the ogre she'd accused him of being, albeit a very handsome one.

"You have to link your little fingers and stay that way until someone breaks it," Fleur explained with not the slightest hint of fear at his sharp mood change.

He was like fire and ice, and she never seemed to know which she might get. Last night he'd been a full-on butthole, this morning he'd shown a little humour and gallantry, and now he was like a stroppy teen who'd had her phone taken away.

"What happens if we don't do it?"

He was talking to Fleur, watching her with a gentleness that squeezed at her heart. No matter what she thought of him, he seemed to care for his niece and was putting her first. It meant hating him was harder than she might have thought, but the remembered look of joy on his face when he looked at Dominique cured her of that notion.

"Then something bad might happen. Like it did with mummy."

Snow placed a hand on Fleur's shoulder in reassurance, hating the sound of fear in the child's voice.

Sebastian stood and he seemed to dominate the large room, making it feel smaller. He crouched beside Fleur, turning the child so she faced him and took her hand in his much larger one. "Fleur, I don't want you to worry about things like that. Mummy was sick before she went to heaven. She would've stayed if she could, and I know she's watching you and loving you from heaven."

Snow was fighting the lump in her throat as he explained to his niece and tried to reassure her without telling her any details that she'd never understand. Snow knew the mother had killed herself but not why and she wanted to know even more now because it obviously wasn't because she wasn't loved by her family or loved her child.

"What if you get sick?"

"I won't because I eat my greens and stay fit."

Fleur nodded and reached out to squeeze her tiny hand around one of the biceps she could see under his white shirt. "That's why you have big muscles."

Sebastian seemed to blush at her words and laughed uncomfortably. "Yes, that's right." He stood and looked at her, the blush still staining his cheeks and she was thrown by the contradiction of the man who was both shy and arrogant at the same time. Yet she wasn't there to understand him, she was there to check on her niece and find out his secrets and if need be, use him to bring down her mother even if it destroyed him in the process. Regret filled her for a second before she cut the thought dead. He wasn't her friend; he was her enemy.

"Shall we?"

Snow snapped from her thoughts to see him holding out his pinkie finger to her. Linking her little finger with his, she once again felt the zing of electricity that had flowed through her yesterday. She'd had a few boyfriends here and there but never anything serious and certainly, nobody that had woken her body and made her ache from such a simple touch. This man screamed danger to every single sense she had, and yet the heady feeling was almost addictive.

They remained locked in the moment both staring at each other his eyes darkening with heat which she knew was reflected in her own.

"Hi ya."

Fleur sliced her hand between them, breaking the connection and the spell he'd seemed to weave over her with such a simple touch. "It's broked now, you can go to work now, Uncy Seb."

As he pulled his gaze away from her, Snow busied herself sorting out breakfast for Fleur and pouring the juice she liked, which was on the sideboard.

"I can, can I, munchkin?"

"Yes."

"Well, okay then." From the corner of her eye, she saw him grab his briefcase and jacket from over the back of the chair, kiss Fleur on the head, and head out the door.

CHAPTER 5

"Snow!"

Seeing the woman who'd infiltrated his thoughts more times than he cared to think about surprised him for a second, throwing him off balance. She looked breathtaking, even with the tiny smudges of tiredness under her eyes she was almost otherworldly.

"Hi, I was just coming to check on Fleur before I head out and get something to eat."

"How was it?"

He stepped fully onto the landing as did she. The smile she gave him was luminous and involved her whole face. It was so genuine and pretty and made her look even younger than her twenty-six years.

"It was wonderful, exhausting but wonderful. Fleur is a very bright child with a lot of enthusiasm for life."

Sebastian nodded, his thoughts turning to his sister, an ache filling his heart that she'd never get to see her child grow up. "Fleur is certainly a handful." A frown crossed his face. "What about letters and words? She gave the last nanny a hard time about learning."

Snow shook her head as she shoved her hands into the pockets of the jeans she wore. "She was fine. We made it into a game and if she gets things right, she wins prizes."

"That's smart. She's very competitive."

A smirk crossed her face and he thought she might say something, but she seemed to hold back.

"What?"

"Nothing, I was just thinking she seems a lot like you in that way."

Sebastian chuckled at her assessment. "I guess she does in that way. I like to win."

"I figured she'll have to work to get rewards in the real world so why not learn that now but in a slightly less aggressive way than real life."

"I hadn't thought of it that way, but you're right, nothing in life is free."

Snow cocked her head and his eyes moved over the elegant curve of her neck. Nothing was provocative about her outfit, not a hint of inappropriateness and he felt guilt edge its way in at the way he'd treated her. It wasn't her fault he was attracted to her, and it had been on his mind what she'd said about Fleur and what he was teaching her.

"Listen, I should apologise about my behaviour the other day. I was rude and out of line."

"But?"

"But nothing. If anyone spoke to or treated Fleur that way, I'd hit the roof."

"Apology accepted."

At that moment her stomach let out a mighty growl and she placed a palm over the flat of her belly, a blush staining her cheeks.

"Sorry, I haven't had dinner and if I don't eat my body is quick to get annoyed."

Sebastian waved a hand. "No, no it's fine. I won't keep you. I just wanted to check-in and make sure everything was going okay." It was on the tip of his tongue to ask her to have dinner with him, knowing Mrs Lewis would've made enough for the two of them but he stopped. He couldn't let this woman become too familiar or blur the boundaries of the relationship he needed to have with her.

He could offer her nothing except sex, and he needed a nanny more than he needed sex. Even if the thought of her naked in his bed, under him, over him, touching him, had been all he could think about. No, he needed to keep things professional. "Well, if that's all, I need to get on."

He didn't wait for a reply, but took out his key for the office, turned his back on her, let himself in and closed the door. Even in there her scent still surrounded him and he moved to the window to open it and let the light perfume leave the room.

Sitting down he put on the glasses he only wore at home when his eyes got tired and opened up his laptop. He had so much work to get done. On top of the trial, he now had to go over the entire report on the judges who'd been found to be in league with Jimmy Doyle, a well-known Irish gangster. He'd been brought down last autumn in a raid when he'd tried to rob the McCullum Estate.

Sebastian had no doubt that there were more people involved than just a few judges and barristers. This seed of poison went deep but then he'd always known the judicial system was corrupt, from the top to the bottom there were people who were willing to take bribes so they could grease their own pockets. It was one of the reasons he'd gone into this line of work and been determined to clean things up.

Removing the glasses, he rubbed his eyes noticing it was already eleven-thirty and he'd once again forgotten to eat dinner. Closing the report, he made some notes on the document he'd opened for just that and then saved it. Closing the laptop he stood, stretching his body on a groan. He needed to get out for a run and clear the cobwebs. Perhaps tomorrow before breakfast he could get in a run, especially as Snow would be there to take care of Fleur. Then he could get back in time for breakfast with them before work.

Relocking the door, he headed down to the kitchen and saw the light was on above the centre island. Snow was sitting there in pyjama shorts and a cami top that showed the curve of her spine as she leaned over the counter dipping cookies into a mug.

"Midnight snack?"

He saw her jump, her whole body moving off the stool and her hand shooting to her chest as she gasped in fright. He stepped forward with a chuckle and crossed to the fridge, trying really hard not to notice the way her nipples pebbled against the silky material. "Sorry, I didn't mean to scare you. I thought you heard me come in."

Snow gave a shaky laugh and looked away from him and back to her cookies, which were laid out in a tower. "It's fine, I was in a world of my own."

Sebastian grabbed the plate of what looked like lasagne and unwrapped it before popping it into the microwave to heat. Leaning back on the counter behind him, he observed the woman who was, despite her detailed work history and background check, a bit of an enigma to him.

"Tea and cookies. Didn't you get dinner?"

Snow wrinkled her nose. "I did, but it turns out I'm a dreadful cook."

"Turns out? Didn't you already know if you could cook or not?"

Snow shrugged an elegant shoulder and the strap on the cami slipped before she could catch it, revealing the swell of her breast and making his dick harden instantly. Thank God the timer on the microwave gave him an excuse to turn away. He jostled the hot plate in his fingers managing to get it to the counter before he ended up wearing it down his suit trousers. When he turned back to grab a fork, she'd fixed her top and was looking embarrassed.

"Sorry, I should have worn something different, but I didn't think anyone would be around at this time of night. It won't happen again."

Sebastian just nodded because he didn't know what to say. Half of him wanted to stride over there, shred her clothes from her body, bend her over the island, and see if she tasted as sweet as he imagined. His body ached just thinking about sinking into her warm heat. The sensible part of his mind made him suspicious that she was playing him in some way, that he was a pawn in a game she was playing to get him into bed and trap him in some way. Although being trapped with a woman like her certainly wasn't a repulsive thought, it was also not something he wanted.

Snow stood to leave, and despite his feelings, he didn't want her to go. He lifted his fork and pointed at her cookie tower. "Finish your snack, it's done now."

Snow slowly slid back onto the stool, and he continued to eat his meal, which could have been sawdust for all he tasted.

"So, tell me about the cooking thing?"

"Well, I lived with my father most of my life, and he was an excellent cook. When he died, I ate with the people I worked with. I make a few meals really well, but it's mostly jacket potatoes, omelettes, and beans on toast."

Sebastian's lips twitched. "God, I haven't had beans on toast in years."

"I can't imagine a man like you ever eating beans on toast."

"What? Of course I have. It's a British staple. I can't imagine anyone not eating it, it's like comfort food."

"I agree, especially with grated cheese on top."

He nodded. "Yeah, the best. I can't remember the last time I ate it."

"I'll make it for you next time I'm making it for myself."

"That would be nice, thank you. But on the subject of your lack of cooking skills, I'll ask Mrs Lewis to start cooking for you when she makes my meals."

Snow stood up and put her hands in front of her before grabbing the mug and her cookies. "It's fine, honestly. I can manage, and you're already paying three times the going rate for this job."

"It's an important job looking after the person who means the most to me in the world. Why would I not pay it sufficiently?"

"I guess, but food isn't necessary."

"Are you saying you don't like Mrs Lewis's cooking?"

He was teasing her now, trying to get a reaction to make her smile at him like she'd had when she spoke of Fleur.

"No, God no. Don't say that. She'd be devastated and she's a wonderful cook. I just don't want to be beholden to you or anyone else."

"Even for food?"

Her reaction wasn't what he expected and made him want to know more about her and why she was so independent. "It's no trouble and if you like, I can add it to the employment package instead of a bonus."

He had no intention of doing that but if it made her feel better, he had no issue with telling a white lie.

Snow bit her lip before nodding. "Okay. That's acceptable."

"Good."

"Well, I'm going to take this and head up. I'll see you in the morning I expect."

Was that a question or a statement? He wasn't sure but he hoped it was a question, and that she was as eager to see him as he was her. Which was damn stupid on his part and would only lead to trouble.

He didn't reply, just nodded, and once again turned away, knowing that watching her walk away in those tiny shorts would be his undoing. He was a man, not a fucking saint, and she was temptation in a perfect package. She was also the first nanny that Fleur seemed to really like and therefore he couldn't afford to fuck this up. Then he realised he hadn't offered his condolences on her father's death and felt like a heel. It seemed he was determined to make a bad impression with this woman.

CHAPTER 6

TWO MORNINGS LATER AND SEBASTIAN WAS FEELING GOOD ABOUT HIS decision to employ Snow. They'd both kept their distance since the night he'd found her in his kitchen in barely anything, the memory still etched on the insides of his eyelids. Any interaction they had was mostly over the phone and regarding Fleur.

A smile creased his lips as his driver pulled up to the courtroom and his offices at seven am. His niece was happier than he could remember seeing her since her mother had died. More than that, she seemed to be thriving, her thirst for life not subdued by sadness and loss and he had no doubt that was because of Snow.

Shouldering the door open, he nodded to Dereck the night guard, who was well overdue for retirement but said he liked to keep busy, lest the loss of his wife took over completely. Sebastian couldn't imagine what it felt like to lose someone you had forty years with but then he'd never met anyone he wished to spend more than a few weeks with. A sudden image of him and Snow came to mind, laughing over the heads of three dark-haired children and he stopped short, almost spilling the coffee down his Tom Ford suit.

He shook off the ridiculous notion. It was clearly time he called someone from his list of suitable partners and got laid. A lack of sexual release and not enough sleep was clearly sending him crazy.

Stopping short as he stepped through the outer office door, he glanced around at the disarray. Papers were strewn everywhere; the desk top computer was broken on the floor and the vase of flowers Margaret kept refreshed every week was smashed on the ground beside her desk.

Dumping everything in his arms on the chair, he raced toward his office, his foot slipping on something as he rushed through the door. Looking down he saw blood smeared over his shoe and horror filled him as he followed the line of it and saw a foot he recognised sticking out from behind his desk.

"Margaret!"

Rounding the desk, he knew the second he laid eyes on her that she was dead. There was too much blood for anyone to survive an attack like that. Still, he crouched to check her pulse, finding her body cold to the touch and her pulse nowhere to be found.

Standing with a heavy heart, he ran back to the main entryway and yelled for Dereck to call the police and an ambulance. He didn't know why he asked for the last, but he wanted to make sure that Margaret was given the best chance, even though he knew in his heart she was already long dead.

As he waited outside his office for the police to arrive, he went through every moment since he'd walked in this morning. Had he passed the attacker? How had Dereck not seen him, and why Margaret? Deep down though he knew this wasn't about her. He'd seen the state of her office and then his. Whoever killed her hadn't been aiming for his long-suffering secretary—no, he would've been the target; he just knew it in a way he couldn't explain.

As the police arrived and sealed off the scene, he was led through to a room beside his as the courthouse was closed down for the day so the crime scene could be preserved, and investigators could do what was needed.

He knew the drill better than most and he still found the entire thing tiresome and frustrating. He answered question after question from the detectives, all of whom he knew on a first-name basis.

'Did anyone have a grudge against him' made him laugh. He was a high court judge, of course they did. Practically every person he'd locked away hated him, but he hadn't had any threats, at least not of late, and those he'd received had been sent to the police and logged as was the procedure.

"Mr Alexander, are you working on anything right now that might make you or your staff a target?"

Detective Chief Inspector Peter Randall was a good man and a thorough and methodical copper who got the job done. He also wasn't afraid to ask questions that could make you feel awkward, and Sebastian respected that.

"I'm in charge of a highly classified report on corruption, but I can't say more without permission from the Home Secretary."

Randall raised a bushy eyebrow and made a note in his burgundy notebook. "I see. Well, we'll contact her office."

He cocked his head and Sebastian braced for the personal questions, but he had nothing to hide.

"I understand you have custody of your niece."

He nodded shortly, not wanting to give away anything he didn't need to. "That's correct. Her mother died six months ago, and I now have custody of Fleur."

"Do you mind me asking how she died?"

Sebastian did mind but he knew as much as he hated it, the man was only doing his job and it was exactly the type of questions he should be asking. "She hung herself."

A look of sympathy passed over the man's face which Sebastian dismissed. He didn't need the sympathy for something that nobody but him could understand.

"And the father?"

Irritation that the wank stain that had sired his niece and ruined his sister's life was even mentioned made him clench his fists. Hate was a wasteful and useless emotion but one he nurtured toward that evil human for what he'd done to his family. That Fleur was the product of such evil, and yet filled with so much light, shocked and surprised him every day. "Is that relevant?"

Randall lifted a shoulder and sighed as he readjusted his bulky body in the chair. "Perhaps? This could be a custody battle gone wrong for all I know."

Sebastian locked his fingers together and let them dangle between his knees. "He isn't in the picture, never has been and if I get my way, never will be. He's not even registered on the birth certificate."

"Do you have his name?"

Randall eyed him, chewed pencil poised to take notes, but Sebastian had no intention of giving him a name. He'd rather take that to the grave than let anyone know the truth about that.

"I don't know, I'm sorry. My sister never said, and I never pushed."

"Hmm." Randall stood and offered his hand. "Thank you for your time and I'm sorry about your secretary."

Sebastian shook it and breathed a sigh of relief that it was over for now. He knew there might be follow up questions but for now, he could go home and hug his niece and make sure she was okay. "When will I be able to get back into my office?"

"Hopefully a few days and the crime scene people will have everything they need."

"Okay, and Margaret's family, have they been notified?"

"Yes, I sent an officer straight over when we confirmed she was dead. We didn't want them finding out from the news, and the media are parked outside."

"Vultures."

"Yes, they are but I guess they have a job to do the same as us."

Sebastian wasn't sure he agreed with that, but he kept his own council on the subject.

Sliding into the town car that would drive him home, he texted Snow to let her know he was heading home early. He'd called to check on them and tell her not to let anyone in the house, and that there had been an incident at work, and she was to keep Fleur away from the windows.

He knew he'd have to give her more details, but he didn't want to let her know about the mess he'd unwittingly dragged her into. He hadn't told the detectives his suspicions because to do so would be to open a Pandora's box that he knew would be impossible to close.

Why couldn't his life be simple? Instead, he'd had to cover up his mother's death from alcoholism to save the family name, hide the fact his father had been a miserable excuse for a husband and father and put more purchase in his golf buddies and his mistresses than his family, and most recently, trying to find his sister's birth parents, while caring for a precious little girl who didn't understand any of it.

Nobody but the family knew that Lucinda was adopted. Nobody except that excrement who'd tortured her with the information for his own sick pleasure and caused her to kill herself out of shame and horror.

That was who he was hunting now, the man who'd fathered Fleur and killed his sister, and most likely killed Margaret looking for the evidence he'd been collecting.

Patrick Dupont, the son of the French President, and the evil son of a bitch he was going to take down if it killed him.

CHAPTER 7

"That's wonderful, Fleur, follow the dots with the pencil."

Snow watched on as Fleur wrote her name using the dots to form the letters and spell out Fleur. It was hard not to show her incredible pride and love for the child she'd only known for a short time. The bond of family was a strange one for her, having only had her father, and their relationship while close hadn't been usual.

It had taken her a long time to figure out that most fathers didn't involve their kids in their robbery plans. Instead of teaching her letters, he'd taught her how to pick a lock in under six seconds or crack a safe instead of riding a bike. Oh, she could do all those things but only because she had a thirst for knowledge and had nagged him until he got a tutor in to help her pass her exams.

No, her relationship with Henri was unique but he'd loved her, and she'd loved him fiercely and she missed him every day, but she'd never want the life she'd had for her own kids—assuming it ever happened. Her current job was hardly conducive to meeting the man of her dreams and falling in love.

Looking out the window at the swing set in the back garden, her mind went to Sebastian Alexander. He was a contradiction and a puzzle, and she found herself wanting to figure him out and make sure his pieces went together as they should, but she couldn't help thinking she was missing a huge part of the puzzle.

He was moody and austere, but she'd also seen the flashes of heat in his eyes when he looked at her that burned her skin. He was arrogant and cold but with Fleur, he was warm and loving, patient and indulgent. Yet she knew from her few conversations with him that he wouldn't tolerate anything but the best.

Her ringing phone brought her out of her thoughts, and she smiled as she glanced at the screen and saw Reaper's name. He was one of her favourite people, always smiling and friendly and she imagined he was what having a big brother would feel like.

"Hey, Reap."

"Morning, baby girl."

He'd called her that since the day they met and it had annoyed her at first but now she saw it for what it was, a term of affection. Not in a sexual way, neither of them felt that way, because he was the brother she never had, and he said she reminded him of his sister. Once sex was taken out of the equation their relationship and the term baby girl hadn't bothered her in the least.

"So, a bit of bad news."

Snow continued watching Fleur, a smile creasing her face as she giggled at something unseen to her. She moved further across the room to look out of the front window, the long expanse of the playroom going from the front to the back of the house, giving her a clear view. She glanced across the road watching for nothing in particular and yet everything at the same time. It was how she saw things most others missed. She watched people and how they interacted and noticed the small things. Like the child who kicked her shoe off as she sat in the pushchair outside the shop on the corner, or the young man who tossed a crumpled-up piece of paper on the ground in anger as he watched a woman in a red coat walk away from him.

"Tell me."

"Margaret Tanner was found murdered in the judge's chambers this morning. She was stabbed three times."

Her attention now fully on the conversation she angled her body away from the window. "Oh no! She was really sweet the few times we spoke. Do we know who or why yet?"

"No, but I'm working on it. From what we know, she was in early as she always is, and her attacker slipped past the guard who was asleep."

"Asleep?"

"He should have retired years ago, but I think they kept him on out of pity. He lost his wife and felt lost so Judge Alexander had him moved to the night shift which was known to be quiet."

"Poor Sebastian, he must feel awful."

"Yeah, not as awful as Margaret Tanner."

Snow chewed her fingernail as she ran through her thoughts and feelings about this new development. She pushed away, her sudden sympathy for a man she'd been fully prepared to hate but found herself more confused by with every moment they shared. "Was anything taken?"

"A laptop from the judge's desk. The rest was trashed. It didn't look like anything else was missing, but only he'd really know that."

"You want me to find out?"

"I think we need to find out exactly what he's up to or involved with. Someone was looking for something today and they killed the person who got in the way of that."

"You think Fleur is in danger?"

The team had been briefed on her relationship with Fleur and to Dominique Dupont. Secrets among Shadow operatives weren't permitted if it affected the job and being caught lying was grounds for instant dismissal.

"I think it would be wise to move up the timeline and find what we need. I also called Bás, and he's sending Titan and Bein down as backup to watch your six."

"What about you?"

"I'm going to stay on the judge, see if I can figure anything out."

"Okay. Keep me posted."

"Will do, baby girl, and stay safe. Don't go falling in love with the judge."

Snow snorted. "Hardly, he hates my guts most of the time and when he isn't glaring at me, he ignores me."

Snow didn't mention the sexual tension, it was hardly relevant and meant nothing to anyone if nobody acted on it.

"Hmm, hate sex is the best, baby."

"Gross."

Snow made a gagging sound as Reaper laughed and the line went dead as was his way. He said he never said goodbye because he'd already said too many in his life and didn't want to end any more conversations with such finality. So, he always just hung up. It was his quirk, just like not swearing was hers. Although hers involved a lot more imagination than simply hitting a button.

Snow spent the next few hours doing puzzles with Fleur, playing games, and finger painting. She knew with everything she should be searching for clues but having an intelligent child follow you everywhere asking questions made it almost impossible. After lunch, she'd settle Fleur with a movie and try and do some snooping then.

But as she finished wiping the table, which Mrs Lewis insisted wasn't necessary, she heard the front door open and close and the air around her prickled with an awareness that only one man seemed to induce. She looked at Mrs Lewis in surprise, playing her part to perfection as she turned to see Sebastian Alexander walking down the hallway. He looked like a juicy steak she wanted to devour in his white shirt, cuffs rolled to reveal strong tanned forearms, a red tie hung loosely at his neck, and an air of exhaustion that tugged at her heart, giving her the strongest urge to soothe the lines of worry from his handsome face.

"Mr Alexander, you're home early. Would you like me to make you a sandwich?" Mrs Lewis asked as he placed his briefcase on the table and glanced around the room as if his mind was elsewhere and he was unsure how he'd got here.

His call just after Reaper's had been short with no details, except to keep Fleur inside and away from the windows. She'd known why of course but hadn't reacted in any way, just telling him she'd do as he asked. His coming home early put a dent in her afternoon plans but there was nothing to be done about it now.

He gave a short shake of his head. "No, thank you. I'm not very hungry."

"As you wish, sir."

His gaze locked on Snow and, as she always did when he focused his attention on her, she felt her body still as if caught in the eye of a storm. He had an intensity about him like the Shadow members did as if he'd seen and done things that nobody would understand or condone. She had no doubt he'd done more than his share of dodgy things to get where he was and stepped on more than a few toes. Watchdog was in the process of confirming it all, but Sebastian was careful and any nefarious dealing he'd done had been cleverly hidden.

Yet in that moment he looked tired and full of regret, and she knew that he felt guilty for what had happened to Margaret Tanner. Whether he was involved in some way or not, he felt responsible and nobody who was truly evil felt that kind of pain or guilt.

Sebastian Alexander had a heart, a big one, he just hid it so well and encased it in so much ice that even he wasn't sure it still beat or if it was truly a frozen piece of tundra. The only person who seemed to thaw the ice was Fleur, and Snow wondered what it would be like to have a man so intense and dominant look at you like you were his whole world. It was a silly and fanciful thought and one she instantly pushed away.

"Fleur is taking a nap. Do you need me for anything before I go and set up this afternoon's activities?"

She didn't know if she wanted him to demand she stay or send her away so she could get her traitorous emotions under control.

His eyes moved over her, not in a sexual way this time but as if he was lost and she was his only anchor in the room. Her hand itched to reach for him, to soothe him, and wrap him in her arms. Her team-mates all said her kindness was both a blessing and curse and she knew Duchess especially worried for her, but she was tougher than they thought. She knew her heart could easily break from trusting the wrong people, but they were wrong.

It wasn't that she trusted people, it was that she read them, and gave everyone the chance to be good, without prejudging them as having malicious intent. Not necessarily a good trait for someone with her job, but it worked for her, and she refused to go through life thinking everyone was evil. It wasn't how she wanted to live her life. She'd rather be sunshine and rainbows than clouds and darkness, even if it bruised her heart sometimes.

"I'd like to speak with you in my office, please."

Snow gave a short nod at his clipped tone and followed as he walked past her, his aftershave swimming through her senses as he did, rendering her lightheaded with desire. The man was a walking lust machine and she needed to shore up her defences if she wanted to walk out of this with her heart intact. Her mind went back to Reaper's words and images of angry sex with Sebastian made her cheeks heat and her body grow heavy.

Sebastian leaned against his desk and folded his arms, crossing his feet at the ankles but he was anything but relaxed, the tension rolling off him and filling the room, so it was hard to breathe. "Close the door."

Snow did as he asked and waited for him to speak, wondering what was going through his mind.

"My secretary, Margaret was murdered this morning in my chambers."

She had, of course, already known the information but hearing him say it, still shocked her. "Oh, no, poor Margaret. Do they know who did it?"

Sebastian gave a short shake of his head before he moved to sit in the chair behind his desk. "No, the police are investigating, but it could be linked to a case I've worked on, so I need you to be extra vigilant with Fleur and of course your own safety if you decide to stay on."

Snow cocked her head, in genuine surprise this time. "If I decide to stay on?"

Leaning back in his chair he again assessed her, and she stayed still, not letting his stare get to her. "You didn't sign up for this, Snow, and I doubt you could fight your way out of a wet paper bag, let alone defend yourself or my niece. That said, she's very happy with you as her nanny, and I'd like you to stay."

Snow worked hard to hold in the swear words she wanted to return at his rude assessment but bit her tongue until it almost bled. However, she couldn't let his words go without any recourse. "I've never fought a paper bag, but I've put a grown man twice my size on his bottom with just a flick of my wrist."

Sebastian's eyes almost glowed with heat as he sat forward, clasping his hands in front of him, a smirk that was both sexy and irritating on his handsome arrogant face. "I have no doubt that a flick of any part of your body could bring a man to his knees, Snow, but I won't have your death on my conscience."

Heat of a different kind hit her cheeks then and it took everything in her not to drag him over the desk and kick his butt. Everyone judged her on her size and the way she looked, and mostly she saw that as an advantage to the enemy who never saw her coming but now, she saw it as the insult it was. "You'd be a fool to underestimate me, Mr Alexander. I may be small and perfectly formed as you so kindly pointed out, but there's more to me than meets the eye."

Sebastian inclined his head as if taking on her point but kept his council as she supposed he must do every single day in his job. "My apologies, Ms Goubert. My assumption was rude and uncalled for. I hope you can forgive me. Today has been very trying."

His apology instantly caught her off guard and had her feeling regret for the way she'd gone at him with her claws bared. "Perhaps we're both a little testy. I'm sure you have had quite a shock today. Would you like me to send some flowers to Margaret's family?"

Her easy acceptance seemed to stun him for a second before he nodded and gave her a tiny almost imperceptible smile. "Thank you."

"You're welcome. Will there be anything else?"

"No, not if you're happy to stay in your current position."

"I am. I love being with Fleur and there's no evidence to suggest we're in danger. However, I'll be extra careful. But if you're concerned, I have a friend who owns a security company who might be able to give you some advice on security or perhaps personal protection for you and Fleur."

It was an off the cuff comment but what better way to get one of the other Shadow members close than to have them here as security. At worst, they could have a look around and see if they could find anything she hadn't had a chance to.

Sebastian seemed to ponder that for a second before he glanced at his laptop and then answered. "Send me their details and I'll look into it. I think some extra cover for Fleur is a good idea."

"I'll email the details over."

A noise from the floor below told her that Fleur was now awake, and she was back on the clock. "That's my cue to go get the teddy bears ready for their picnic. Feel free to join us later if you wish. I'm sure Fleur would be happy to extend you an invite."

Her lips curved up at the warm look on his face and her heart gave an involuntary jump. She'd need to watch herself with this man or she'd lose sight of the objective and that couldn't happen. A little angel's happiness was on the line, and she wouldn't let her down as all the adults in her own life had done.

CHAPTER 8

H<small>E HADN'T PLANNED TO, BUT</small> S<small>EBASTIAN HAD DECIDED TO TAKE A FEW</small> days off. The case had been adjourned for a few days until they could determine that the defendant or his cohorts weren't involved in any way in Margaret's death. He'd holed up in his office the last two days working on his sister's family secrets and finding a way to bring down Patrick Dupont that didn't implicate him in the process. Not that he cared if he went to prison if it meant an end to the man, but he had Fleur to think of.

He was her only family now and he wouldn't do anything to jeopardise her safety or happiness, and life in the system, while he was in prison, would be hell. He'd worked enough cases to know there were good people out there, but he also saw the worst of people and he wouldn't risk that she'd be one of the unfortunate ones, or worse, somehow end up with that evil bastard and his mother.

Taking off the glasses he wore when he got tired, he rubbed the bridge of his nose where a headache was beginning to form. The light was starting to dim as the day began to end and he realised he'd once again secluded himself away from the person who needed him most.

Fleur was a bundle of joy and energy and every time he looked at her, he was reminded of his sister and her zest for life. They'd been so different, him staid and controlled, her so free and wild and yet they were close, and he'd loved her and missed the life she brought into his dull existence. Growing up the way they had forced them to be co-conspirators in so many ways, but he'd been the big brother and a proud one too. In the end, though, he hadn't been able to help her find her way through the pain and depression that had marred her life like a black cloud, only lifting at brief times to let the sun shine through her so bright it was blinding.

Standing, Sebastian stretched his tight muscles, his shirt lifting over his abs just as the door to his study flew open and Fleur rushed inside followed by a harassed looking Snow. He hadn't seen her much since their exchange the other day and he drank in the sight of her now as she let her eyes wander over him, a blush staining her cheeks pink before she seemed to snap out of it.

"I'm sorry, she took off like a rabbit."

He smiled and crouched to his niece who threw herself into his arms. Sebastian stood with her in his arms and turned his attention to Fleur. "And what can I do for you, munchkin?"

"I want to watch a movie and eat popcorn and I want you to do it with us." Her eyes moved to Snow who was watching them with a strange warm look on her face. "Snow said we could build a fort and watch a movie under there on the laptop."

"Is that so?" His gaze returned to Snow, and he noticed the way the simple blue cotton dress she wore hugged the curves that were usually hidden. She wore hideous black biker boots on her feet and the combination on her seemed to work. She was so far from his type as to be laughable but whenever he was around her all he could think about was how she might taste or feel beneath his hands.

"I told Fleur you were busy, but you know how it is when an idea takes root."

He did know and at the moment she was the idea he couldn't shake. "I do and I have the time. But I need food first, I forgot lunch."

"Yes!" A little hand of triumph shot in the air at his easy capitulation, and he tickled Fleur's tummy making her giggle.

"I could reheat some of Mrs Lewis's lasagne for you?"

"Or we could order pizza." He glanced at Fleur to see the look of approval on her face and knew it was the right call. Bending, he set her down on her feet. "Go sort the fort for us in the den and I'll order the pizza."

His niece ran to Snow and slipped her hand into hers, dragging her toward the door. "Come on, he said yes. We need to build it before he changes his mind."

That comment, said so innocently, hurt more than he thought it would and he vowed to spend more time with his niece and not cancel his plans with her.

Following behind them, he could hear them laughing and talking in the den as he took the menu from the kitchen drawer. He had no idea what Snow liked and went to ask her only to find her on her hands and knees, her sexy ass in the air tempting him in a way he didn't need but couldn't seem to walk away from.

"Ms Goubert, what would you like on your pizza?"

A flushed face looked up at him, her hair escaping the braid she wore it in, and she wrestled with the sheet. "Anything, I'm not fussy."

Sebastian went back to the kitchen to place the order and while there he took a call from the man Snow had suggested he use for his security. He'd checked them out and their credentials were impeccable with no red flags of any kind. "Mr O'Scanlan, thank you for calling me back."

"I'm sorry it took me two days. I was in the US on a case."

"It's fine. I'm not altogether sure I need your services, but my nanny gave me your number after an incident at my office." Sebastian went on to tell the man about Margaret and his job and his concern for Fleur.

"I agree caution is a good idea. A person with your profile, and especially with your job, is always going to be a target for people wanting revenge or idiots seeking to make a name for themselves. Has there been any direct threats or any concerns you haven't mentioned?"

Sebastian knew he couldn't reveal anything else to this man, he didn't know him well enough, and the Duponts were highly respected around the world. "Nothing to speak of and nothing in the last few years, but it's not my safety I'm concerned about. I have custody of my niece and she means everything to me."

"In that case, I'd recommend a PPO, a personal protection officer and a full security review."

Sebastian knew what both of those were, having worked in the criminal justice system long enough. "How soon can you get someone over to see me?"

"I'll send two of my men down first thing in the morning. Is nine okay?"

"Yes, I'll be working from home until the middle of next week."

"Mr Allen and Mr McCullum will see you then."

Sebastian hung up feeling like he was doing the right thing for his family, and somehow in the last week that had begun to include Ms Goubert. She was getting under his skin, and he wasn't sure what to do about it, having never suffered from such an affliction before.

The fort was uncomfortable, cramped, and he felt ridiculous, and yet the smile on Fleur's and Snow's faces made the cramp in his leg worth it. With Fleur cuddled between them on the large cushions from the couch, laughing at something Buzz Lightyear did on the screen, he relished this time knowing his sister would never get to experience it.

His eyes caught on the curve of Snow's neck, how it sloped down with elegance and grace into the swell of her breasts that teased him. The dress was perfectly appropriate, and he was ashamed of his behaviour when they'd first met. None of what she wore was to tempt him and to anyone else, it wouldn't even cause a second glance but on her, it set his blood to lava and made his skin prickle with need. Perhaps it was just her and the spell she'd cast on him from the very beginning.

At that moment she turned and gifted him the most radiant genuine smile he'd ever been on the receiving end of and if he hadn't been sitting on his ass, he'd have staggered back from the effect.

He knew she had secrets, but she also had an innocence to her that called on the most protective part of him. As their eyes locked, he could feel everything fall away around them, as if they were the only two people in the world and whatever connection was arcing between them seemed to hold them both in its spell.

The air seemed to sizzle and flicker, and he knew if it wasn't for Fleur, he'd have her nanny on the cushions while he pleasured her until her only thought was him, until he consumed her in a base way. He knew the risk would be that she'd then own parts of him he wasn't prepared to give away, but he wasn't sure he could stop her from stealing them if she so wished.

Fleur tapped his face, forcing his attention to her and he broke the connection that had made his heartbeat like a drum.

"Can we watch more?"

Sebastian lifted Fleur onto his lap and kissed her head. "No, princess, it's time for bed, but maybe we can make this a regular thing. Friday night is movie night."

"Yes." The little girl clapped her hands, the action making him smile, something he'd done more in the last six months than in his entire life.

"Why don't you put Fleur to bed, and I'll clean up down here."

He glanced at Snow and was grateful to have found her, not just because Fleur liked her but because he did too. "Thank you."

Fleur pouted. "I want you and Snow to put me to bed together."

He frowned, about to shake his head. "How about I come up after I've cleaned up and give you a quick story and then you go straight to sleep. You have ballet in the morning."

"Are you taking me?"

"No, I have to run a few errands, but we can do something after if you want?"

"Okay, fine."

Sebastian smothered a chuckle at his niece's long-suffering tone and tried not to think about what the errands might be or if she was meeting someone. Jealousy was an ugly emotion and not one he'd ever suffered from, and he certainly had no right to feel it toward Snow. She was nothing to him, just the nanny, an employee like Mrs Lewis was. Even as he thought it, he knew he was full of shit. Everything about this was different, he just didn't know how or what it meant yet.

Striding for the stairs he tossed Fleur over his shoulder fireman style and relished the belly laugh that erupted from her "Come on up the apples and pears."

"You're funny, Uncy Seb."

"And you're a rascal pants. Go get your pyjamas on and brush your teeth and I'll be in to say goodnight."

Parenting a child you hadn't raised from birth was a strange and tricky road to navigate. He felt the need to give her privacy for certain things like changing, even though he knew if he'd been her father, he wouldn't have even thought of it. In this day and age when everything and everyone was evaluated as a pervert, he found himself being extra cautious and not overstepping a boundary that might make Fleur uncomfortable.

"I'm ready."

He poked his head in and saw her sitting up in bed, her arm around Pumpkin, her teddy, toothpaste smeared on her chin. A smile creased his face as he went to his knees by the bed and leaned on the quilt covered in pink unicorns. Her room was typical of her age, with pink everywhere and dolls and teddies on every surface. Never had he imagined this would be his life and the transition from bachelor to full-time parent had been a steep learning curve but one he found he enjoyed.

There was an innate innocence and joy in children that fed the soul with hope, and in his job where he saw the worst of humanity on a daily basis, it was easy to lose hope and become jaded. Fleur had changed that; she'd given him a different outlook on life that he'd been lacking. That didn't mean there weren't days when he was overwhelmed and exhausted from the responsibility. He had no idea how single parents did this without help and it gave him a new respect for each and every one of them and he hoped would make him a better judge.

"So, what story would you like?"

"I want one of Snow's stories."

The little girl pointed behind him and he saw Snow leaning in the doorway watching them, an indulgent look of what was almost love on her face. For a second, he wondered what life would be like to have a family, a nucleus of a mother, father, and child. How that tight-knit unit would fight the world for each other.

Snow moved closer, her dress swishing around her toned thighs and knelt beside him on the floor, her scent spilling over him in a wave. He should move away but the pull was too strong.

"One story. Then straight to sleep, okay."

Snow was firm with Fleur, but she tempered it with genuine affection and care, almost like a mother would and again he wondered what life would be like if he shared it with another, or more especially her. The thought shocked him, and he went to move, to get away from the confusing, uncomfortable presence of the woman who was turning his world upside down without even seeming to try.

A little hand grabbed his arm and he stilled. "Stay, Uncy Seb."

Every instinct in him told him to run, to get away from this minx but the imploring look from his niece stilled his retreat and he reluctantly settled back on the floor.

As Snow told her story of ice warriors and snow fairies who fought against the evil Ice Queen, weaving magical characters and amazing feats of bravery into each line, he fell under her spell, enraptured by the tale as much as his niece. Her voice was lyrical and full of life, her excitement in every word.

By the time she was finished, Fleur was fast asleep, her breathing even as Snow tucked her covers more securely around her body and dropped a kiss on her head. He felt her leave the room as he checked the window was locked in the child's room, caressed her fine hair back from her face, and switched off the lamp leaving only the night-light to cast a warm glow on the room as she slept.

In the den Snow was clearing away the rest of the fort that had been their cocoon from the world. She looked up, a smile in her eyes, and he found himself frowning in irritation. What hope did he have against her when she gave away her joy so freely?

"Is she asleep?"

"Yes."

He saw her flinch at his terse tone and regretted it almost instantly. Again, she was making him change who he was without a word. He was this way with everyone and had never had any compunction about it. If people didn't like who he was, or the way he was, then they could remove themselves from his vicinity, but he found himself wanting to be better, softer, around her.

"Go to bed, Snow. I can clean up."

"It's okay, I don't mind."

In a second he was across the room to her, grasping her wrists to his chest in his much larger hands, forcing her to drop the sheet she was folding. Her eyes shot to him, and he didn't see fear in her big blue eyes—only heat and longing that shot lust to his aching cock. He was teetering on the edge of a decision that could break him in ways he didn't fully understand but sensed like prey sensed a preda-tor. No, that couldn't be right. He was the predator here although he felt like prey to the allure of this woman.

A pulse beat in her neck, her eyes flared with desire, and he could feel the electricity between them as if it had a life of its own. Her pink tongue came out to wet her bottom lip, and the need to taste her and feel her softness was so strong he almost groaned.

Bending, he ran his nose along her neck, his lips barely skimming her flesh in a whisper, the skin like silk. He inhaled her scent, felt the pulse beat against his lips, heard her breathing change, and knew she was as affected as he was. His teeth nipped the sweet skin behind her ear and his legendary control was close to breaking as she shuddered against him, her hands and body relaxing into him.

Then the mood changed in an instant. He felt the way she closed down before she yanked from his grasp with no difficulty at all. Not that he'd have stopped her or was holding her tight, but the movement was a practised one, which made him wonder about her earlier comment of putting him on his ass.

They stared at each other for a breathless moment, the air stilling as if it too was waiting to see what would happen. He saw a myriad of emotions cross her beautiful face, each one fleeting and mirroring his own. Sebastian knew if he pushed it, he could have them moaning in pleasure in his bed in minutes, but he'd never forced or coerced a woman into his bed, and she was the last woman he should even be considering there.

"Go to bed, Snow, before one of us does something we'll both regret."

She stared at him for a second as if deciding if she'd heed his warning then turned her back and walked away from him. It took everything inside him not to follow and finish what he knew they both wanted.

As he lay in bed that night flitting between regret for making things awkward and wondering if he should just say to hell with it and take her to bed and get it out of their systems, there was one irrefutable fact and that was he'd been right about Snow changing his life. He just still hadn't figured out how yet. One thing he did know was that he'd have her in his bed screaming his name, and when she did, she'd be the one coming to him, he wouldn't chase her.

CHAPTER 9

THE MORNING AIR WAS CHILLY AS SNOW WALKED TO MEET REAPER. HE'D said he wanted to discuss the case without the threat of little ears hearing but she knew he was really checking up on her. When he'd called to check in last night she'd still been reeling from the heated encounter with Sebastian. While she could hide her emotions from most, Reaper and Duchess always saw through her, which was annoying and sweet at the same time.

Reaper was sitting in the window seat of a coffee shop near the park, his apparent preoccupation with the racing slips in front of him all a ruse. She knew he'd clocked every single person in the room and evaluated whether they were a threat before he even sat down. She also knew he was aware of her walking toward the door because she saw the slight fall of his shoulders as they relaxed.

The young woman behind the counter glanced up and smiled as she walked in, and Snow returned her unspoken greeting as she moved to join Reaper. With his tan skin and blond, almost golden hair, he attracted attention from women wherever he went. Nobody could deny he was handsome, in a surfer boy way and the Australian accent made him almost impossible to resist for old and young women.

Snow noticed the young woman's smile fall as she sat across from Reaper. She tried to hide her grin as she took off her denim jacket and laid it on the seat beside her. "Still breaking hearts, I see."

Reaper glanced up, a half-smile creasing his lips as he glanced sideways at the woman behind the counter and winked.

Snow groaned. "Do you ever turn it off?"

Reaper leaned back, placed his arm across the back of the chair, and assessed her. "What can I say, when you've got it, you've got it."

"Whatever."

At that moment a second waitress she hadn't seen before came from the back with two plates. Both held a full English cooked breakfast. She also had mugs of coffee on the tray and placed them in front of Snow and Reaper with a flourish.

"Can I get you anything else?"

Reaper shook his head. "No thanks, Holly. This looks great."

The woman preened under his praise and Snow fought the urge to shake her head at his antics. Reaper was harmless and never hurt any of the women who seemed to fall endlessly in love with him by promising things he couldn't deliver. He was just one of those men who women fell in love with and ended up a lasting, sweet memory in their lives, even after he left.

Snow tucked into her breakfast with gusto. She hadn't slept well. It always made her hungry and there was nothing like a full English to fix her woes. As she shovelled fried bread and bacon into her mouth, she forced her brain to ignore the memories of her encounter with Sebastian that tried to play on a loop inside her brain. She'd lain awake most of the night trying to make sense of her mixed emotions when it came to him.

She'd come into this thinking of him as the villain she needed to protect her niece from and had soon discovered he was a devoted uncle who not only put Fleur's welfare first but was open and easy with his affection for the child. That Fleur adored him was a testament to how good he was with her. That didn't mean he wasn't a bastard in every other avenue of his life, and he was certainly hiding something. His involvement with Dominique was evidence of a dark side he hid from Fleur. No man who could smile at that woman could be trusted.

"What's going on with you?"

Reaper's voice broke into her thoughts, and she realised he'd been watching her for a few minutes as he drank his black as tar coffee.

Guilt assailed her at the memories of the way Sebastian's lips felt on her skin, of the way he'd made her forget everything but him for just a few seconds before the reality had come crashing back in and she'd run from him. Retreat wasn't like her, but she was self-aware enough to know that if she'd stayed, lines would've been crossed that they couldn't come back from.

The problem was, in lots of ways and without knowing his history with Dominique, she liked him. He had integrity in his job, seemed to take care of his staff, even if he was cool and stuffy. But seeing him with Fleur was what really made her heart soften toward the arrogant asshole.

"Nothing is going on with me."

Reaper leaned forward on his elbows and looked at her intently. "Why would you possibly think you could lie to me, baby girl?"

"I'm not lying." Even she could hear the snark in her voice and winced inwardly at the dead give-away.

"Is it the judge? Do I need to kick his ass?"

Snow reached to place a hand on Reaper's arm to quell any worry he had for her. "No, Sebastian is fine. I can handle him."

"You sure? 'Cos Bein and Titan are meeting with him now. I can call them and they can fuck him up a bit for you."

Snow laughed and shook her head. "Don't be ridiculous. He hasn't done anything untoward."

"But he's done something?"

Snow sighed. Knowing she had to give him something or he'd harp on at her like an old woman. "We nearly kissed."

Reaper leaned back silently, his eyes moving to the people who walked on the pavement outside. His jaw in profile was square and rigid, his brows a slash on his forehead and she waited for him to speak. That was the thing with Reaper, he was never quick to react, always taking the time, no matter how long or short, to get his thoughts and feelings in order. His ability to not react without thinking things through, every scenario going through his head like a film, was probably what had made him such a good Special Forces operator.

Finally, his eyes came back to her and in the warm, blue orbs, she saw concern for her. "I won't try and tell you how to behave or feel because despite me seeing you like a sister, I know you're not a child. But be careful, Snow. We don't know enough about this man and although you say he's good with Fleur, and I can't deny from what I've witnessed that's the truth, he's still a cutthroat businessman with a lot of secrets."

"Is there any other kind?"

"Probably not, but his could get someone killed and remember, you're the one who wanted to go after him to get to Dominique Dupont."

Just hearing her name made the hackles on her neck flare to life in irritation. Her utter hatred for the woman who'd birthed her was almost a living thing inside her. Throwing her aside like trash wasn't enough, that she'd then come back into her life and had stolen the only person who'd ever loved her, took her hatred to a new level.

"I know, and I haven't lost sight of the goal. It's just chemistry, that's all."

"Mmm, maybe. Just be careful. I don't trust him. I don't think he had anything to do with Margaret's death, but he's up to something."

Relieved Reaper was letting it go she zeroed in on his subject change as she sipped her milky coffee sweet with two sugars. "Do we have any leads on that?"

Reaper shrugged. "A few, it looks like the man who killed her is a knucklehead who was just out for some cash. He showed no finesse and it was a messy kill."

Snow tried not to show any emotion as Reaper spoke of Margaret, the sweet woman who'd talked about her family on the very first call they'd shared. The fact was, she needed to be less emotional about this entire case. She had no trouble with any other, but this was different and she knew it. It was probably why she was reacting to Sebastian the way she was. "Any names in the mix?"

"Watchdog caught him on CCTV leaving the scene. His name is Jakub Nowark. He moved to this country eight years ago from Poland. He works as a bouncer at a nightclub in Soho. He has a criminal record for petty theft, grand theft auto, and assault and battery. He served two years in his own country for a serious assault on a man he worked for at a garage in a dispute over pay."

"Sounds like a real charmer."

"Oh, he's a peach."

"Do the police know?"

"They do, but we need to try and find him before they do. We need to know who he's working for because there's no way he's behind this."

"Do you think Sebastian was the target?"

Reaper pursed his lips. "Possibly, but he seemed to be looking for something."

"The laptop?"

"Maybe. Either way, I think it's a good call to have backup and increased security. Nowark won't stop until he has what he wants. He's in debt up to his eyeballs to some very bad people and my best guess is this is how he pays that debt."

"A gun for hire."

"If his accounts are any indication, then yes. He had ten grand deposited the day Margaret was killed from an account Watchdog is still tracing."

"Fine, keep me posted." Snow stood to leave and dropped some cash on the table, making Reaper frown.

"Come on, just this once let me pay."

"No fucking way."

He took the cash, and knowing she wouldn't take it back, dropped it in the tip jar before he settled the bill himself. Snow put her jacket back on, the September air already cooler than a few weeks before. It wouldn't be long before the shops were decked out in all their Christmas glory. She wondered what it would be like to spend Christmas with Fleur. To see the delight and joy on her face and share the magic of it all with someone so innocent. She couldn't ever remember being so innocent and Christmas had been a very different affair for her and her dad.

As he met her on the pavement, Reaper pulled her into an uncharacteristic hug and kissed her cheek before pulling away and dipping his head to her hair as she laughed at his sudden affection.

"Be careful, baby girl."

Snow patted his cheek. "I will. Now go take your charms else-where before you break more hearts."

His grin was infectious, and she watched him walk down the street, one second there the next gone as if he truly were a ghost.

Snow walked the short way home, deep in thought about the situation with Sebastian and Fleur. On the one hand, she wanted him to be everything she'd thought he was so she could justify her actions and the lies she'd told but on the other hand, she wanted to believe his heart was good. That under the hard, cold shell he showed the world was a good man. The same man who showed Fleur such love and gentleness, the same one who'd turned her inside out with lust and need.

Putting the key in the lock she jumped when the door was yanked open before she could get inside. As she stepped back in surprise, almost losing her balance on the step, Sebastian's furious face came into view as he caught her arm saving her from a tumble down the stone steps.

"Sebastian?"

He held up a finger to silence her and her surprise turned to anger at his overbearing ways. "Don't fucking speak, right now, Snow, or I swear to God, I'll put you over my knee and spank your ass until it's raw."

His hand on her bicep, he marched her toward his study and closed the door firmly behind them, encasing them in silence and an energy she couldn't describe.

Pulling her arm away, she moved across the room and turned to face the red-hot anger she could see on his face. "What the hell is wrong with you?"

Sebastian was breathing hard as he paced the room like a caged tiger, his movements controlled and smooth. His angry eyes moved to her, and she felt scorched by the heat in them and embarrassingly turned on by the way he was watching her and the thought of him following through on his threat of spanking her ass.

"Me! What is wrong with me? Well, let me see, maybe it's because my employee, who I trust with the most precious thing in my life, has lied to me."

Snow felt her heart beat faster. He knew. *Oh shit* somehow, he'd found her out. "What the hell are you talking about?"

Sebastian stalked closer and she fought the urge to step back, knowing that to show any weakness to this man was a mistake he'd exploit. "Don't lie to me, I saw you with him."

Now true confusion coloured her thoughts. "What?"

Sebastian was standing so close now she could feel his warm breath on her skin, sense the energy coming from him in waves. "The man in the café this morning. The man who held you close as you said goodbye, who touched you."

Realisation dawned on her and with it the knowledge that Sebastian had followed her. Snow lifted her chin in defiance and saw his nostrils flare with heat and anger. "You followed me?"

"Of course not. I was driving home from Fleur's ballet lesson and saw you together."

The harsh slash of his brow deepened, and Snow had the sudden urge to laugh. He was jealous. "Are you jealous, Mr Alexander?"

Sebastian flinched as if she'd struck him. "Don't be ridiculous. Why would I be jealous? I just don't like my employees lying to me."

"I have no clue why you'd be so green with envy at seeing me, your employee who you explicitly warned away from you, with another man." She saw a muscle in his jaw tic at her words.

"Exactly, because I'm not. I'm just angry it wasn't mentioned in your interview when I asked you."

Snow leaned in slightly and poked him in the chest. "I don't mention it because I don't have a boyfriend. Not that it's any of your business but the man you saw me with is a friend, a good one, and I wouldn't touch you if you were the last man on earth." She now knew that Reaper had hugged her on purpose, somehow having seen Sebastian's car going past and trying to elicit a reaction in him. She'd need to speak to Reaper about that, find out what the hell he was playing at.

Sebastian stepped forward so his chest was almost touching hers when he breathed out, and the air thickened around them until it was almost suffocating. His hand lifted and she stilled, not in fear but anticipation, her eyes closing as he skimmed a finger down her cheek like a feather caressed by a breeze.

"You got a few things wrong, Snow. Firstly, it is my business. I own you. Secondly, if I wanted you, I could have you and we both know it."

Her eyes flashed open on his arrogant declaration but instead of seeing the cocky, aloof man, she saw heat and desire so deep it made her bones ache. She did want him, she could admit that to herself, but not to him. Sebastian Alexander was the kind of man who took and took until there was nothing left. While she knew the journey would be heaven, the end result would be disastrous for them both. Only she knew the true extent of the way their lives were entwined so she needed to be the one to take the step back. "Nobody owns me and as for having me," she did air quotes with her fingers, and he wrapped his hand around her left one bringing it to his chest, and she could feel his heart beating as fast as her own and it made her want him so much more than she ever should, "we can't, Sebastian. Too much is at stake, and you said yourself I'm not your type. You hate me most of the time and tolerate me for the sake of Fleur the rest. Sex would just muddy the mix and it would end badly."

Snow knew she'd all but admitted to wanting him, but now wasn't the time for games when there was so much to lose for both of them. She watched his face, saw the battle that raged, felt his hands warm on her skin and desperately wanted to throw caution to the wind.

Sebastian stepped back, dropping her hand, and putting space between them, the air around her feeling cold at the loss as he turned his back to her. "Don't lie to me again, Snow. I can handle most things, but I won't tolerate liars."

"I understand."

As he left the room, allowing her to breathe again since the angry storm that was Sebastian Alexander had whirled into her, she wasn't sure if she'd dodged a bullet or missed out on the best sex of her life. The truth was probably both.

CHAPTER 10

"Please, Uncy Seb." Fleur looked up at him through long dark lashes and he wondered absently if this was built into the female DNA, the knowledge of how to wrap a man around your little finger with a single look.

"Fine, let's ask her and see if she's free, but if she isn't, you need to stop nagging me."

He'd promised Fleur a trip to the Zoo and even with everything going on he wasn't going to break that promise unless it was absolutely necessary. Having spoken to Mr Allen yesterday, while the other guy had checked his security and made some recommendations, he'd deemed it safe to be out as long as it was in public places. Nothing was more public than London Zoo on a sunny Sunday.

"Yay!"

Fleur jumped up and down with excitement and Sebastian shook his head in defeat. After his awful behaviour yesterday and his complete over-reaction at seeing with her another man, no, not another man, a man. She wasn't his as she'd pointed out, and he found the thought unsettling because he wanted her to be. He'd avoided her the rest of the day, making excuses and she'd seemingly done the same, eating in her room instead of with them, claiming tiredness.

He needed to apologise to her and assure her he was done being an asshole but where she was concerned, he found his normally strict behaviour was unpredictable. The problem, he found, was that not only was she the most effortlessly beautiful woman he'd ever met, but she was also sweet and kind. She also had a hidden core of strength running through her that drew him to her like a moth to a flame. Above all that, she seemed to love Fleur as much as he did.

All last night he'd been full of regret for a second night and still, he was torn between wanting to run from her and wanting to hold her close and never let go. Him, a man who used willing women for their mutual pleasure, was thinking about commitment and it was terrifying. Especially given that he'd never even kissed her, and they'd spent most of their time fighting. Yet bickering with her was more of a turn-on than fucking most of the women he'd been with.

The air in the kitchen changed and he knew before he turned around, she was there.

"Snow."

Fleur jumped from her chair and ran to the woman who was dressed in skin-tight ripped jeans and a pale green top with yellow flowers on it. White chucks on her feet gave her a girlish look that was betrayed by the sexy curves that wouldn't let up. Her ice blonde hair was pulled into a simple ponytail and her face had minimal make-up. She was breathtaking and if he was another man, he'd go on bended knee and beg her to stay with them, but he wasn't. He was Judge Alexander, and he didn't beg for anything.

He watched Fleur bouncing with excitement as Snow crouched to her level, which wasn't far considering she was so small herself. "Hey, sweet pea, what has you so excited?"

"Uncy Seb is taking me to see the lions and the sloths."

Her eyes moved to his and he saw hesitation and caution there as well as approval. He'd never sought approval from anyone, not since he was a child trying to please a father who'd never care enough to give it, yet he found himself feeling ten feet tall at hers.

"That sounds fun."

"Will you come? Pleeeeease?"

Sebastian smiled as Fleur drew out the word as if doing so would give it more impetus.

Snow glanced at him in question, and he saw the hesitation again and knew this was his doing. He'd fucked up and needed to fix this, for his niece's sake if nothing else.

"We'd really like it if you could join us."

He could still see her wavering, so he implored Fleur's tactics.

"Pleeeeeease?"

Snow burst out laughing and it lightened the room and made the ice around his cold heart thaw just a fraction more.

"Well, how can I ignore such heartfelt invitations? I'd love to come with you."

"Yes!" Fleur punched the air in delight making them both laugh as their eyes caught on the shared moment.

"We should get going."

Sebastian stood and grabbed his keys from the counter. Allen and McCullum were coming first thing to upgrade his security and he reminded himself to tell Snow later. He didn't want to ruin their day by telling her now and reminding her of the danger he'd dragged her into.

London Zoo was heaving with people, from young couples on romantic dates to families and busloads of tourists. It was his usual idea of a living hell, but as he held Fleur's hand in his with Snow holding the other, swinging her between them, he found he was enjoying himself.

They'd seen the lions and the sloths and were headed toward the reptile house when he saw a woman walking toward him with a barely concealed look of rage on her face, which she quickly masked. Sebastian wanted to groan at his bad luck. Of all the people and all the places, he had to run into Julianne Talbot.

She looked immaculate as always, her dark hair in loose artful waves around her shoulders, her make-up flawless. Even her clothes screamed money, with her designer black trousers and cream cashmere Bardot top that was completely out of place on a trip to the zoo.

"Sebastian, fancy seeing you here of all places."

"Julianne."

He saw her eyes flash to Snow with such hate that he wanted to step between them and shield the smaller woman from the harsh, razor-sharp tongue he knew Julianne had.

"Aren't you going to introduce us, Seb?"

Seb? Since when had he allowed her to call him that? Even when he fucked her, he'd been Sebastian. The only two people who called him that were Fleur and Lucinda. He bit his tongue wanting to get this over with and made the introductions. "Snow, this is Julianne. Julianne, this is Snow." He left out who Snow was to him. He knew in his heart it was way more complex than her just being the nanny at this point, just not how and he wasn't prepared to explain it to this parasitic woman.

"Nice to meet you."

Julianne gave a weak smile and Snow the once over. He knew she was finding flaws where there were none. Julianne was a snob and bitch, and it was only seeing her there now that he saw what a climbing, conniving bitch she was, which she proved with her next statement.

In flawless French she addressed him without a glance to Fleur, further confirming his lowering opinion of her. "Really, Sebastian, you threw me away for this piece of trash?"

An ice-cold rage fell over him at the way she was trying to exclude Snow from the conversation. He was so livid at her words he could barely get any words past his lips. It turned out he didn't have to, because Snow, who he'd forgotten was French, so used to her slight accent now that it had ceased to exist, replied in her own flawless French.

"Oh, honey, he didn't throw you away. I told him to take out the garbage if he wanted in my pants, and it turns out I'm that good at deep throating him he doesn't even care that I'm using him for his money." Snow looked Julianne up and down. "And let's face it, you can't polish a turd and call it a diamond no matter how hard you try."

Julianne gaped like a fish and turned suddenly, spinning on the heel of her stupidly high boots as she did.

Sebastian couldn't help it; he threw his head back and laughed before wrapping his arm around Snow and kissing her head. "Marry me!" The words were said as a joke but as she looked at him with wide eyes for just a split second, he wondered what a life with a woman like her would be like.

"Ha-ha, you couldn't handle me, buster."

He released her with a smile and put some space back between them. "I think you might be right."

Fleur, who'd been oblivious to most of what was said, was getting bored, so they headed to the reptile enclosure where she proceeded to beg him for an alligator as a pet. That had involved tears when he'd said no, and he realised she was probably hangry.

Like him, when his niece got hungry, she became irrational and as she tucked into chicken nuggets and chips and he ravaged a bacon burger, he reflected on how much he was enjoying his day with them and how he wished it wouldn't end.

"Uncy Seb, are you going to marry Snow?"

His niece looked up at him with innocent eyes and he almost choked on his burger as his eyes flew to Snow who was trying to hide a laugh behind her napkin. Her twinkling eyes telling him he was on his own with this one.

Sebastian chewed his food to buy himself some time and then wiped his mouth before facing his niece who was looking at him too intently. "Well, um, no. Snow is your nanny and my friend."

Fleur cocked her head to the side. "But you asked her, I heard you."

Shit, he'd thought he'd got away with that stupid throwaway

comment but now it was biting back hard. "Yes, I did say that, but it was more of a joke."

"Don't you like Snow, Uncy Seb?"

He could see the sheen of tears in her eyes now and felt himself flailing to make her understand without breaking her little heart. "Of course I like Snow, she's very nice."

"And pretty."

Sebastian nodded, feeling like a bear caught in a trap. "Yes, and pretty."

"And you kissed her head like you do me, which must mean you love her too."

A strangled sound came from Snow, and he glanced across to see her almost crying with laughter at his predicament. He scowled at her, and she laughed harder, and he wondered why, when grown men were terrified of that look, she had no fear in her whatsoever. Maybe it was because she knew he'd never lay a finger on her in anger.

"It's different, Fleur."

"Why?"

God, why did his niece have to be so damn smart?

"Your Uncle Seb and I are friends and sometimes friends joke and show affection. It doesn't mean he wants to marry me or that he loves me the same way he would a wife or girlfriend."

"But he asked you."

"Yes, he made a bad joke, which I'm pretty sure he's regretting right about now." Snow took Fleur's hand in hers and traced a pattern over her palm making her laugh, the threatening tears forgotten. "It was just his way of saying thank you for getting him out of a tough situation."

"You mean making the bad lady leave?"

"Yes, I helped make the bad lady leave and he was glad, so he made a bad joke."

"Adults are funny."

Snow laughed and hugged Fleur. "Yes, we are."

"Will I be funny one day too?"

"No, you'll always be perfect, my little angel."

As Sebastian watched the two together, relieved that once again she'd hauled his arse out of the fire. He wished she wasn't his nanny and he was the marrying kind because a lifetime with Snow in his bed and by his side sounded like something he wanted.

As they finished walking around the zoo, looking at the penguins and flamingos, Sebastian felt an idea begin to grow in his mind. He liked Snow. Having her in his bed certainly wouldn't be a chore, not with the amount of passion she had, and in the few weeks they'd known each other, Fleur loved her, and she seemed to feel the same.

He knew he couldn't offer her love, not because he couldn't. He loved his niece and his sister, even his mother. He'd never again give away that kind of power to another and allow them to hurt him in the process, but he had other things he could offer her.

Was marriage such a silly idea? Lots of people made marriages of convenience work, more they flourished. They could give Fleur stability, love, security, and Snow could have financial security and whatever else she wanted.

Not one to make rash decisions, despite the evidence to the contrary lately, he knew he'd need to sleep on it for a few days before he broached the subject. Perhaps speak to his lawyers first and draw up a prenup agreement.

As SNOW PUT Fleur to bed, he headed for his office and sent an email to his lawyer, telling him he wanted a meeting asap. Then he returned a call from the lead detective investigating Margaret's murder. Bitter sadness assailed him at the thought of the woman who'd been his right hand at work for so long. She'd been more than a personal assistant; she'd been like a surrogate mother in some ways. Handling way more than was expected of her, even fending off his ex-conquests with a smile and a pot of tea. He hated that it had taken her death for him to see that and appreciate her. He was a man who hid behind walls so high sometimes he wondered if he was protected or trapped.

"Judge Alexander, thanks for calling me back."

"My apologies for the late hour. I was at the zoo with my niece."

"No problem, I know how young'uns are and it's good to spend time with them. They grow up so fast."

"Yes, they do."

Sebastian didn't dislike this man, but he had no desire to make small talk with him either. "You have an update on the case?"

"Yes, we've arrested Jakub Nowark for her murder."

Sebastian didn't know him but that wasn't unusual, he dealt with so many people it was hard to keep track of them all. "Do we know his motive?" The leather of his desk chair creaked as he sat forward, arms braced on the desk.

"No, we believe it was a paid hit."

His belly clenched with the knowledge that he'd been unfortunately right, and this was linked to him after all. If this was a paid hit, then Margaret hadn't been the target, it had been him. "I was the target." It was a statement, not a question and they both knew it.

"We believe so. So I ask again, is there anybody specifically who'd want you dead?"

Sebastian knew he couldn't involve the police in this. It would be buried in red tape, with the potential for political scandal smeared all over it. He was honestly surprised his actions hadn't tipped off MI6 or, as it was now called, the Secret Intelligence Service. He needed to speak to his contact, the man who'd approached him and started this hateful, but he'd thought necessary, witch hunt.

"Throw a dart around me and you'll find someone who wants me dead. My job doesn't exactly imbue love and devotion from the people I put away."

"I'm aware of that and we're looking into that but if you think of anything specific, let us know."

"Yes, I will and thank you for the update."

"You're welcome."

"Have you released the body to the family yet?"

"No, not yet, but we will sometime this week according to the coroner."

"Thank you."

Sebastian hung up, his mood dark after that call. He rubbed his thumb over his bottom lip, thinking of everything he had going on. He knew something was going to have to give and he knew it should be his vendetta against Patrick Dupont. Yet just the thought of what he'd done to Lucinda made his blood boil with rage. He needed to pay for what he'd done, and his mother needed to pay for covering up his evil for so long that she'd become implicit in who he'd become.

His father had always said power was key, that the more you had the more protected you were, but he knew different. He had power yet most days he felt powerless to protect the person he cared most about.

Revenge was what ruled him most days although today he'd given that over to joy and the simple pleasures of just being and enjoying the moment, and he couldn't remember a time when he'd felt so free.

If he had Snow, would he still feel free or would he merely drag her into his personal prison? The truth was he didn't know, and he shouldn't care. He hardly knew the woman but that didn't stop him from thinking of her as he stroked his cock in the shower to ease the ache in his body. It didn't stop him from imaging what she'd feel and taste like as he fucked her mouth and pussy. As his hand moved faster, he pressed his hand against the shower wall to support his shaking legs and came so hard he saw stars, his release covering his hard abdomen and hand.

Cleaning up, he dressed in loose sweats, learning quickly after Fleur moved in that sleeping naked was a thing of the past and went to check on his niece. She was sleeping soundly, a sloth plush under her arm as she slept the sleep of the innocent. Walking back to his room, he stopped at the base of the stairs leading to Snow's room, wanting so badly to go to her and find out if his imagination was as good as he thought or better.

He didn't though because he was a man who made choices and didn't allow his emotions and hormones to get the better of him. He was a man, a Supreme court judge, and he decided when and how and who.

CHAPTER 11

Snow placed her phone on the bedside table and sighed. The police knew about Jakub, which meant they'd soon find out he was just a hired gun. They all knew Sebastian was the target, which was why, despite what Titan had told him, Sebastian had a guard twenty-four-seven. She'd spotted Reaper and Duchess, who was still working the Cavendish case with Bishop in London, at the zoo, but thankfully Sebastian didn't see them, which was their job. Nobody was better than her team at blending in and disappearing.

She'd also spotted Titan and Bein, but they were too good to allow Sebastian to see them. She was grateful for them being there to protect them. Her niece was precious to her, and it was nice to know that others had her back as she walked around the zoo like a normal person just enjoying the day. Her guard was still up, it was as natural to her as breathing but she'd been able to enjoy herself more knowing her friends were watching out for them.

A wave of affection assailed her for the men and women she called friends when, in reality, over the time she'd been with them they'd become so much more. They were a family with Bás as the overbearing and annoying father of the group. With Bein getting hitched to Aoife soon, that family would be extending, and she was happy for him. They were stupidly in love, and it was difficult to be around them without feeling that intense adoration between them both.

Turning on her side, a smile creased her lips as she remembered the look on Julianne's face when she'd replied to her in her own native tongue. She'd looked like she might pass out from the sheer shock of someone daring to say such things to her. Snow had known who she was immediately, it was in the file she'd read on Sebastian. She'd shared his bed for a while and the knowledge and seeing her try and claim the man had set Snow's claws to sharpening.

His reaction had been priceless and the sheer joy in his laugh had made her breath hitch. Sebastian was a handsome man. GQ cover model handsome, and with the beard he was growing, he was even more so, but when he laughed with such freedom it was like the world stopped turning.

Flopping back onto her back she felt restless. Although she was bone-tired from not sleeping well, her mind simply would not shut down. She could go down and make some warm milk, but she ran the risk of running into the very man who was keeping her awake. Something had changed the last few days and she was seeing him less as the enemy and more as an ally. She had no evidence to back up her theory that he was a good man, except what she saw with him and Fleur, but her instinct was screaming at her that there was more to this man than what he showed the world. At times it was like he was a wounded animal who still nursed an old injury and wanted to protect it with all his might.

Sitting up she grabbed her phone from the side and started scrolling through social media, finding herself on his Instagram page before she realised what she was doing. There wasn't a lot of pictures and none of Fleur, which she was happy to see. He clearly valued his privacy, which gelled with what she knew of the man. Seeing he'd been tagged in a few pictures, she clicked through and was rewarded with a drool-worthy shot of Sebastian on a boat somewhere in the

Mediterranean if she wasn't mistaken. His blue swim shorts clung to his wet legs, and it looked like he'd just hauled himself from the sea. His body delivered on everything it promised under those white dress shirts he wore. Tan, warm skin, rippling six-pack abs, leading down to the irresistible V that made her want to take a bite out of him. He had a smattering of hair on his perfect chest and his dark hair was swept back from his face as he smiled at the camera. A stab of jealousy pierced her belly as she wondered who he was smiling at. Noting the date was two years ago, she scrolled through more pictures to see two other men, both with girlfriends or dates but in every picture, Sebastian was either with them or alone. It was irritating how much that made her relax.

Sebastian wasn't hers to fawn over or get jealous about. He was a means to an end, though even the thought made her feel sick. Deceit was part of her life, she'd grown up thinking lies were normal, that they didn't hurt people. Only as she got older, and her own moral compass had begun to grow did she realise how wrong her father was.

Lies still formed her life. With the job she did, even she knew some were imperative to save lives and keep people safe, but this felt wrong to her. She was lying to Fleur too and she knew Sebastian wouldn't forgive her.

On a whim, she sent a text to Duchess asking if she was awake. Her phone rang in her hand, and she smiled as she answered.

"What's wrong?"

Snow shook her head even though her boss and friend couldn't see her. "Nothing is wrong."

"You sure? I can come over and kick the hot judge's ass for you."

Snow laughed at her friend. "The hot judge hasn't done anything."

"Well good, because I've been walking around on four-inch fucking heels all day and my feet are killing me. I swear a man invented them to torture women."

"Wear flats then."

"Can't. Heels make my ass look great in a pencil skirt and Carter Cavendish likes to ogle me."

"Isn't he the one you're trying to bring down with his brothers' help?"

"Yes, Gideon and Damon are helping but Damon is being a pain in my ass."

"How?"

"He keeps getting all overprotective and trying step between me and what I need to do to get Carter talking."

"He likes you."

"Hmm, well he needs to stay out of my way."

Duchess was beautiful on another level, with long dark glossy hair, warm tan skin, and a plethora of tattooed artwork on her arms, thighs, and chest, even up her neck. Her green eyes popped and were winged, giving her a constant sultry look. Men literally fell around her like flies and she didn't even seem aware half the time.

Half Italian, Duchess, real name Nadia Benassi, spoke six languages and was learning more constantly. She had a fiery temper to match her Italian roots and had links to the original Sicilian Mafia. More than that, Snow wasn't sure of. Like her, until now, they all had personal secrets that only Bás and most likely Jack, who'd recruited them, knew of.

In a fight, she'd always bet on Duchess though, against anyone, man or woman no matter how big. She was deadly and sexy, which was a combination that was priceless in their job.

"So enough about me, what's got you calling me at this time of night?"

"Technically, you called me."

"Whatever."

Snow heard a horn beep and music in the background. "Where are you anyway?"

"In a posh bar in the West End watching Carter schmooze some poor woman. It actually makes me want to vomit. She can't be more than eighteen and is drinking up his poison with a straw. Now stop stalling."

Snow sighed. She knew she was stalling but she still didn't know what she wanted to say. "I want to tell Sebastian who I am."

"What?"

"I need to tell him who I am to Fleur. Not about us but my relationship to them."

"Why?"

Snow shrugged even though her friend couldn't see her. "I don't know, I just don't like lying to them both."

"The kid I get, but why do you care what he thinks of you?"

"I don't know, maybe because he has custody, and he could make it hard for me to see her if I piss him off."

"You could fight him."

Snow was shaking her head. "I don't think I could, she adores him, and he dotes on her and anyway, who is going to give me custody over Judge Sebastian Alexander?"

"Um, good point. Your career is hardly conducive to child-rearing."

"Exactly."

"If you tell him, he could throw you out and jeopardise your case and everything you've been working towards."

"I know, that's why I called you."

"You want me to tell you what to do?"

"Yes."

"As a friend, I say tell him. If this is making you anxious then get it over with and see where the chips fall. As your boss, I'm saying don't tell him. You're perfectly placed right now to get the information we need and to get close to him and find out what he's up to."

"Well, that helps."

Duchess laughed and it was deep and sultry, just like the woman herself. "Listen, just think it over and don't do anything rash. Perhaps give it a few days and then we'll talk again. Perhaps really decide what it is you want and why you feel so conflicted. I think if you're honest it has more to do with Sebastian than Fleur."

"Has Reaper been talking to you?"

"No why?"

Snow shook her head. "Nothing, just something he said."

"You know what the Aussies are like, always messing with people but I'll say this, he loves you like a sister. So if he's worried about you, then he's seen something you haven't."

"I can take care of myself, you know."

"We do know that but tell me this. Have you ever been conflicted before this case, which is personal on every level?"

"No." Even Snow could hear the sulky tone in her voice.

"See, it's complex so no rash decisions. Keep doing your job and we'll talk in a few days."

"Okay. Thanks, Duchess."

"You're welcome. Now go to sleep. You have a four-year-old to look after tomorrow."

Snow laughed softly at the shudder in Duchess' voice. "Night."

"Night Sweetie."

Snow hung up and lay back in her cosy bed, the light from the skylight bright blue from the half-moon. Duchess was right, she needed to keep doing her job. Even though the deceit didn't sit well with her, she'd have to take the risk and see what hand she was played.

Checking her gun was loaded and close by as she'd done each night since she was old enough to shoot, Snow cuddled into the cream quilt and fell into a light sleep.

CHAPTER 12

Sebastian was startled awake, his heart racing, eyes gritty as he sat up in bed. Looking at the clock he saw it was just past two am and he'd only been asleep an hour. Swinging his legs out of the bed, he was about to touch the floor with his feet when he heard the sound again and froze.

Someone was in his house, and if those footsteps were any indication, it wasn't Snow. One thing he noticed about her was that she could walk into a room, and he'd have no clue she was there until she made her presence known. It was uncanny and slightly unnerving, but he knew those steps didn't belong in his house this night.

Standing as quietly as he could, he pulled on some old trainers and grabbed the cricket bat he kept for just such occasions and tiptoed to the door. He needed to get to Fleur and Snow and make them safe. At the last minute, he grabbed his phone and saw he didn't have a signal.

He was about to step foot into the upper landing when his door opened slowly. Hiding behind the door, he lifted the bat over his head, ready to bring it down on the intruder. His heart was racing with adrenaline and the need to protect the people he loved the most in this world.

As the person slipped past the door, he made to swing until the bright blonde hair caught his eye from the light of the moon and he mis-swung, catching air instead of her pretty little head. Snow turned at the same time, a weapon he'd never known she'd had aimed at his chest. Relief shot through him, quickly followed by shock as she dropped the weapon to her side and scowled at him.

"Jesus fucking Christ, Snow. I could have killed you," he whispered angrily.

"Don't be silly, I'm the one with the gun."

"Which we'll talk about at another time."

"Yes, we will, because two men are inside your house. My guess is they're armed and dangerous and we both know you're the target. We need to get to Fleur and get her out of here."

"The phone is out."

"Probably using a signal jammer."

Sebastian frowned, wondering just who the hell this woman was because she wasn't the sexy nanny he and Fleur had spent the day with. No, this woman was cool and focused and said words like signal jammer. He didn't have time to ask any of the hundred questions now running through his head as another sound from downstairs reached his ears.

"I'll go first and cover you. I want you to get Fleur."

Sebastian felt his eyes bug out of his head at her suggestion that she protect him and cover his house. It was his house, and he was the man here, he'd do the damn protecting. "No way, you get behind me."

He saw the effort it took her to rein in her temper as she sighed with control. "Look, Sebastian, there's a few things I need to tell you. One of which is I'm perfectly capable of taking care of myself and this situation. But we don't have time for your hero complex right now. I have the gun and Fleur is more used to you. You can carry her easier than I can. So do as I blinking ask."

He had no time to respond before she was opening the door and heading out, her gun in front of her like she was in an FBI show. No, not like, exactly the same. Her stance was calm, steady, and she cleared the landing and watched the stairs like a pro. Knowing he had no choice, he ducked into Fleur's room and found her fast asleep her sloth still under her arm.

Crouching, he lifted her into his arms with her blanket and spoke into her ear. "Munchkin, we're going on an adventure, but I need you to do as I say and stay really quiet. Keep your head tucked into my chest, okay."

"Is it a game?" Her voice was full of sleep and yet she accepted his every word as if he was God.

"Yes, it's a game."

Fleur followed his instructions, and as he stepped onto the landing and glanced at Snow who was looking at him, he heard the first shot splinter the wood of the bannister beside Snow. His adrenalin pumping, his gut told him to dive in front of her and protect the woman who'd chewed him up in knots, but his arms were full of the only other person who could do the same.

"Shit, go."

Snow pointed toward her room where he knew a fire escape ran from the back window. He took a second as he watched her fire back at the people shooting at her with the calm precision of an experienced firearms user. A groan and the sound of someone falling snapped him from his shock and he did as she told him. Snow was clearly more than she'd portrayed herself to be and right now he was clever enough to know he wasn't in control there, she was. As much as that grated every nerve in his body, he'd take it because Fleur's safety came first.

"Go, I'm right behind you."

Sebastian gave her one last look before he headed upstairs, a whimpering Fleur cradled in his arms. He dropped a kiss on the child's head as he took the steps two at a time.

"It's okay, munchkin, just some loud noises."

"I don't like it."

"Me either," he muttered to himself.

To get to the fire exit, he had to go through Snow's bedroom, which was tidy and clean, evidence of her only in the scent that hung in the air. More shots coming from downstairs had his anxiety rising, and the urge to turn back and make sure she was okay, to put himself between her and the damn bullets meant for him, was strong.

Lowering Fleur to the bed, he went to the window and leaned out to open it wide, cool night air rushing inside. More shots coming from downstairs had him feeling torn and impotent; two things he never felt.

He wasn't a man to run from danger and especially not one to leave a woman alone with armed gunmen to face it alone. But as he looked at Fleur, who was quickly realising it wasn't a game and saw the fear on her innocent face, he knew he didn't have a choice. Either way, he'd hate himself for what he did next.

"Come here, munchkin." Lifting the child, he stepped out onto the metal stairs and looked down to make sure nobody was lying in wait for them. With the large patio area clear, he began to slowly climb down.

A commotion below him had him looking down and he saw a man pointing a gun at him and Fleur. Frozen, he knew he was a sitting duck and had no weapon of his own to fire back, at least not on him. His own secret gun was locked away and as useful as a chocolate teapot right now.

As he said a silent prayer to a God he didn't believe in, he closed his eyes and turned Fleur away in the hope that he could shield her long enough that Snow or someone could get to her. Surely someone had called the police already, gunfire was hardly commonplace in this area.

As he ducked his head and rounded his shoulders to try and make himself a smaller target, he heard the discharge of a weapon and waited for the agony to spread through his body, but only heard the thud of something below him.

Turning, he saw the man who'd been hugging Snow outside the café, a gun in his hand, standing over the man who'd been about to kill him. He looked up, his features a cold mask of focus he recognised as the same as his own.

"Move before you fucking get shot."

With no choice but to trust him, Sebastian rushed the rest of the way down the stairs.

"Where's Snow?"

"Inside. There are more of them. I don't know how many."

"There's a car out front. Get inside it and wait there."

With a cool look of disdain he understood as being for leaving Snow, the mystery man ran toward the side door.

Sebastian had no choice but to do as he was told. He was the underling here and the child in his arms was his priority. Seeing the black BMW X5 with blacked-out windows, he made his way toward it and saw Mr McCullum, the man from his new security team in the driver's seat. He jumped out to get the door and ushered them inside, closing it behind them. He turned in his seat and beamed at Fleur.

"Hey, beautiful, do you want to go on an adventure?"

Fleur cuddled closer to him, and Sebastian wrapped his arm around her tightly, his focus out of the window looking at his home which was shrouded in darkness. Not knowing what was happening was torture. He had so many questions he needed answering, not least, who the hell were these people and why were they helping him and how was Snow involved? Because an itch at the back of his neck told him she was no nanny.

The seconds ticked on, and he kept his eyes on the house willing the woman he'd been considering asking to be his wife to come out. He glanced at McCullum in the rear-view mirror and watched him shake his head once and glance at Fleur.

Sebastian understood his desire not to talk in front of Fleur and felt the same energy radiating off him as he had the other blond guy.

"Uncy Seb, I don't like this game."

Sebastian kissed his niece's head. "I know, munchkin."

The man in the front turned in his seat and smiled at Fleur who smiled back, shy for the first time in her life. "Are you a Paw Patrol or a Teen Titans fan?"

Sebastian was watching Fleur as she lit up as this clearly dangerous man, who he knew had a gun on his lap as his other hand held the steering wheel, spoke her language.

"I like Ricky Zoom."

He smacked his hand to his forehead and rolled his eyes making her laugh. "Of course you do. A smart girl like you likes to work out puzzles and save people. Well, think of this as a grown-up Ricky Zoom. We have a mystery and you're gonna help solve it."

"What about Snow?"

Sebastian felt his gut clench, worry making bile rise in his throat. If something happened to her while she was protecting him and Fleur, he'd never forgive himself.

"Snow will be fine. She's a secret superhero. Shh, don't tell her I told you."

Fleur's eyes went wide. "She is?"

"Yep. So you need to be brave like she is, okay?"

"Okay."

With that little chat, Fleur's bravery was restored, and Sebastian felt even more inept than before.

Looking at the house, he knew it was only a few minutes, but it felt like hours since he'd seen her face down gunmen for him. He wanted to yell at her and bend her over his knee and spank her ass raw for being so stupid, for putting herself in danger for him, a man who didn't deserve her loyalty or sacrifice, but he also wanted to drag her into his arms and kiss her senseless and thank her for protecting Fleur.

The car revving caught his attention and he glanced out of the side window to see Snow and the other guy running toward them.

Snow jumped in beside him in the back as the other guy took the front seat beside McCullum. The scent and sight of her healthy and breathing sent relief shuddering through him as Fleur threw herself into Snow's arms. He wanted to do the same but held back.

As the car tore away from the house he loved, which had been the scene of a gunfight, he wondered how his life had come to this. The soft silk touch of fingers on his arms made him look to Snow over Fleur's head.

"You okay?"

Her touch sent fire through him, every thought from earlier coalescing into one as he gave in to the urge and wrapped his arm around both her and Fleur.

"I think that's my line, Snow."

"I'm fine. Just a couple of nicks from some broken glass."

Sebastian rubbed his thumb over a smudge of blood on her cheek, revealing a cut that didn't even make her wince but made him want to turn the car around and go back and find the men who'd done this and do what he should have done the first time. Instead, he held her closer.

She didn't try and pull away from his hold but nestled deeper into it, kissing his niece on the head as if to reassure herself she was okay.

"We need to send a clean-up crew."

The man who'd saved his life turned in his seat and looked at them, assessing the way he was holding Snow. Sebastian tightened his hold, his gaze not wavering in the slightest. He didn't even know why he was laying claim to a woman he didn't even seem to know, let alone know if she liked him at all, or if he even liked her now that he knew she'd lied. It was instinctive and territorial, and he knew he was being a dick.

Apparently, that was the side of him she brought to the fore, and he wasn't going to fight it when this blonde god was looking at him.

"Titan is handling it," McCullum responded as he wound his way through the streets of London.

"Where are we going?" Sebastian finally found his voice after the last twenty minutes of complete mayhem.

Snow refused to look at him. "A safe house."

"Safehouse? Who are you people?"

Snow glanced at Fleur who was snuggled between them, sleeping already. "Let's talk when we get there."

"Fine, but then I demand answers to what the hell is going on."

"Seems like we all have some questions that need answering, hey, Judge."

"Don't, Reaper," Snow warned the blond man he now knew went by Reaper of all things.

He shrugged his shoulders with a smirk. "Fine, baby girl. You handle it."

Reaper calling Snow baby girl made him want to rip his pretty-boy face off and pound it into the ground. A growl escaped his throat and Reaper's smirk seemed to go up another infuriating level. Fuck his life. He didn't know whether to hold her closer or wring her damn neck!

CHAPTER 13

Snow watched Sebastian as he settled Fleur in the big double bed at the safehouse. It was a cute, detached cottage just outside London in Reading. It had easy access to Oxford Road and a good visual around the property. More importantly, it had all of Shadow Elite's security set up and couldn't be traced.

Bein and Reaper were downstairs updating Bás and Duchess via secure video link, and she was up stairs, not concerned with the two lives she'd ended but terrified of the cold shoulder Sebastian was giving her. When she'd heard the men break into the house, her gut had clenched with fear. Her only concern was to get Fleur and Sebastian to safety.

Revealing she was more than who she said she was, had flown from her mind in the midst of the fear almost drowning her. As Sebastian had run up the stairs with Fleur in his arms, leading her to safety, she'd seen the internal battle that raged in him. He wanted to protect her and Fleur. It was natural for an alpha male like him to protect those around him, and especially one like Sebastian who craved control in all areas of his life.

Even knowing she'd have to answer all the questions she saw in his eyes, she knew it was worth it to keep them safe. Now it was time to pay the piper, and she was scared for the first time in a really long time of disappointing someone.

When she'd got in the car and seen and felt the relief move through his body as he wrapped her and Fleur in his strong arms, she'd thought it would be okay. Yet now the danger was over she could feel him pulling away. His walls, the ones he'd been beginning to lower toward her, were back in place and the cool aloof man she'd met turned to face her.

"We should talk."

He gave her a sharp nod, his shoulder straining against the top he'd borrowed from Bein, his jaw so hard she was worried he'd shatter his tooth enamel. His arm brushed her nipple as he moved past her through the doorway and she held her breath, her traitorous body betraying her at the light, innocent touch. His scent and close- ness sent sparks of desire through her body, fanning the flames of lust she was finding harder and harder to fight against.

Sebastian flinched and she knew he felt it too and was far from happy about it. A sigh filled her chest, and she knew this was going to complicate everything. Her budding attraction to the man she wasn't even sure she liked some days was making her head swim.

"Let's go sit outside. The air is warm and we can talk without Bein and Reaper hearing."

"Fine."

Sebastian held out a hand for her to go first, his old-fashioned manners and etiquette bred into him, even when he wanted to strangle her or at least she thought he might want to. Snow led the way past the living room where Bein and Reaper were still talking, knowing she should be on that call, but wanting to fix this, whatever this was, first. Reaper would update her later anyway.

The air was warm enough that a light jacket over her thin t-shirt was enough, her legs that had been bare from her sleep shorts were now covered with leggings. All the women of Shadow were roughly the same size, except for the fact she was a fair bit shorter than the others. Still, the clothes they kept there were good enough. She led him to a bench that overlooked the fields of green as far as the eye could see during the day. A stream that she couldn't see but could hear, tinkled in the dark of the night as it edged toward the orange grey as the sun and the moon swapped places.

Sebastian sat down next to her, two feet between them as if he didn't trust himself any closer. The ease with which they'd been communicating was now gone. "So, talk."

A spur of anger flickered in her blood at his cool tone, and she tried to keep in mind he was in shock. "My name really is Sabine Goubert, and my nickname is Snow. I can't give you the details of the people I work for, but I can say that we mean no harm to you or Fleur."

"Oh, well, that's okay then!" Sebastian angled toward her, the sarcasm and anger vibrating off him.

"Sebastian, I know you're angry and what happened was terrifying for you and Fleur but please listen."

Sebastian linked his fingers together and went back to watching the sunrise, the bursts of orange and purple, slashed with vibrant pinks and blues bathing the world in a beauty only a few got to see each day.

"I'm listening."

"We took an interest in you because of your involvement with Dominique Dupont. We had a case last year that brought to light her dealings with a man named Jimmy Doyle."

Sebastian glanced at her, his sharp jaw covered in a dark scruff she itched to feel on her skin. "The Irish mobster?"

"Yes."

"Wasn't he killed in a gunfight in Scotland?"

"Yes, he was. As you know very well, the investigation into him led to a number of high-level politicians, judges, and law enforcement officers being suspended, pending further investigation."

"I was led to believe the arrests and subsequent investigation was being done by British Security Services."

His frown made her want to swipe her thumb over his brow and smooth the wrinkles away. How could she explain this without giving away everything that Shadow was? Secrecy was imperative to the very existence of the team. Aoife had only been told the full details after her engagement to Bein.

"The Security Services aren't involved but the operation has been sanctioned by the highest authority in the land."

She could see he didn't really understand but was trying. "Okay, so how do I fit in? Surely you could have asked me why I was involved with Dominique."

Snow cocked her head. He made it sound simple, but it was far from that. "Would you have just told us?"

Sebastian had the grace to look sheepish. "Probably not."

"Look, I know you have secrets that involve her, and I also know who Fleur's father is." She held up a hand as he went to speak, his face paling a little. "I know that Patrick is her father, and you'll do anything to protect her from him and his mother. I get that, but you need to be honest about this and tell us what you know."

Sebastian stood abruptly and began to pace the undirected anger and fury rolling off him in waves. "Lucinda was beautiful, so sweet and kind, but she had awful taste in men. I guess as her older brother, I'd said that too often because when it came to Patrick, she just wouldn't listen no matter how hard I tried." He shoved his fingers through his hair, giving him a just fucked look that Snow really liked. He was so tortured by this she could feel his pain and regret as if they lived and breathed.

"When she got pregnant, he promised her the world and his mother seemed to welcome her with open arms, but I knew the rumours about him being a sadistic bastard who liked to play games and never trusted any of it. Lucinda persuaded me to go and meet them to get to know them. So I flew to France with her and stayed for two days at the Chateau in Cap Ferrat on the French Riviera."

Snow knew the place, having studied it many times from the satellite images and in person.

"There was nothing overt, but there was an undercurrent of sleaze and slime about the whole set-up. I knew Dominique was as fake as a two-quid Rolex and Patrick made my belly crawl, but Lucinda was happy, so I played along."

"Did Dominique ever say anything to you that made you suspicious of her motives or her son's?"

Sebastian looked at her as if really seeing her and she fought the urge to go to him. An affection that had crept up on her so quickly she was blinded by it, wrapped around her heart for him.

"No, nothing obvious. She had lots of visitors, some I recognised and others I didn't. A few of the ones I recognised made me wary of her. In my line of work, you learn quickly who the bad ones are. They have a certain veneer about them that is easy to recognise."

"Is that what you saw in Patrick and Dominique?"

"Yes."

"Then what?"

Sebastian closed up, his body turning to her against the backdrop of the rising sun casting him in light and shadow which made him look like he'd been painted by the masters. He was a beautiful man, not just his face and the body but the way he held himself, the way he could dominate a room, fill it with his mere presence. "I think it's time for a bit of quid pro quo."

"What do you want to know?" Snow itched to clap her hands between her knees but knew it showed weakness and now wasn't the time to seem weak in any way.

"Why you? Why go undercover as my nanny? You could've found out so much more from being in my office or just pretending to like me. I would've fucked you long before now if you weren't meant to be caring for Fleur."

She knew he was lashing out to hurt her and it worked, his barb hit the mark making her wince. His eyes went dark against the dawn light, and she saw a flash of regret before he seemed to swallow it down like cheap brandy.

She could lie and tell him any number of things, but he deserved the truth if she was going to expect it from him. "Cheap shots are beneath you, Sebastian. I'm a lot of things but my body isn't for sale for money or this job."

Sebastian sniffed, showing his disbelief and she wanted to hit him, to wound him like he was wounding her. Standing, she walked to him where he stood at the edge where the patio met the lawn and poked his magnificent chest. "I wouldn't fuck you if you were the last man on earth." The lies spilling out angrily with each poke made her cringe, but she held fast.

Sebastian grabbed her hand, stilling it against his hard chest and she realised how close their bodies were. She could feel the hard press of his erection against her belly. His breath feathering her skin made her want to breathe him in and sink into the sensations she knew he could give her. Her nipples peaked like diamonds begging for attention and her core clenched with aching need.

"I could lay you out like a fucking picnic on this grass and feast on you until you screamed my name, and you wouldn't lift a finger to stop me."

"Your arrogance is not attractive, Mr Alexander."

"That's Judge Alexander and your lies are only believed by you, Ms Goubert. We both know if I was to slide my fingers inside your underwear right now, I'd find you soaked for me."

Her clit spasmed, desperate for his attention for him to do the things he was saying but she held still, the moment so charged between them only they existed in this time.

"Are you projecting Judge Alexander?" Snow couldn't resist shifting her weight just the tiniest fraction to rub against the length grazing her belly.

Nostrils flaring, Sebastian glared at her, neither willing to lose nor wanting to look weak.

She heard the back door slide open and took a fraction of a step back, but Sebastian's hand stilled her movement, holding her where she was in a possessive move, she hated to admit she liked.

"Baby girl, the kid is awake."

Reaper's voice reached her, and she could have sworn she felt the rumble of a growl slip from Sebastian's throat.

"Fucking Aussie."

Snow ducked her head to hide her grin and turned from Sebastian to Reaper, who was wearing his own grin. "Thanks, we'll be right there."

Reaper walked back inside, and she went to follow.

"This conversation is far from over, Snow, and I *will* get my answers."

Her step didn't falter as she went through the door with Sebastian at her back. She knew the truth would come out, even if she wished for a second it could be shoved back inside Pandora's box.

CHAPTER 14

After wasting an hour giving Fleur her breakfast and avoiding Snow, Sebastian knew he needed to speak to her team or whoever the hell they were and find out what they knew and what the plan was. After his initial relief at seeing her safe and the protective instinct that had come over him in the car, he'd felt the anger and betrayal creep into his mind until he was almost shaking with anger.

To think he'd been on the brink of asking this woman to be his wife. Yes, out of convenience and companionship, but it had involved a hell of a lot of trust. Something she didn't deserve and had thrown away by lying to him and wheedling her way into his life. He got the feeling he still wasn't fully aware of the reason. What he couldn't understand was the feeling of hurt that was lodged in his gut. Anger he could understand but her lies hurt him in a way he hadn't expected. Perhaps because she'd disappointed him and shown him how things could have been, yet it was all a lie.

"If you're through sulking, we have some things to discuss."

Sebastian glared at Reaper who just smirked back. His hands clenched with the need to ram his fist down the other man's throat. Sebastian gritted his jaw and took a second to compose his features before he turned from Fleur, who was sitting at the table drawing, to look at the man they called Reaper.

Sebastian didn't know what it was about him that rubbed him the wrong way, but everything he did annoyed him, and what the hell was with him calling Snow baby girl all the time like she was his possession in some way. Only the fact that he'd saved his life made Sebastian decide to bite his tongue, but that wouldn't last forever. "Fine."

"We'll be in the living room when you're done. Bein can watch Fleur. He loves to get his nails painted."

Fleur's head shot up as Bein walked in, giving Reaper a sharp dig in the ribs as he walked past, muttering asshole low enough that Fleur never heard him.

Fleur was almost bouncing in her seat with excitement at the prospect of painting the man's nails. "Do you really?"

"Sure, my nieces always love to paint my manly nails."

"Can I?"

Bein crouched to Fleur and Sebastian watched closely, not trusting anyone with his niece right now.

"Well, we don't have any polish, but we can do some drawing together while your uncle Seb and Snow talk with Reap. When we get a chance, I'll let you paint my nails. How does that sound?"

Fleur cocked her head, pursing her lips and giving the idea some serious thought. Seb was impressed with how patient Bein was as he waited for her to respond.

"Okay."

Bein sat down beside her and grabbed a crayon, waving them away with his free hand.

In the living room, Snow was waiting by the window, her body tensing as if she sensed them in the room before she turned with her usual wide smile on her face. Sebastian wondered what it took to put a chink in her sunny disposition, annoyed that she could smile when his world was turned upside down. As he looked closer, he realised her smile didn't reach her eyes the way it usually did, and his heart ached at the loss he'd just seconds ago wanted.

"Take a seat, Sebastian."

Snow sat on the sofa and Reaper took the seat beside her, making him grit his jaw as sudden explosive jealousy reared its ugly head, making him want to rip the man away from her. Instead, he took the single seat opposite them and waited.

"The men who attacked you last night are colleagues of Jakub Nowark."

Snow was leading this meeting and Sebastian was entranced with her confidence as she took charge, her words hardly making a dent.

"Nowark?"

"The same man who killed Margaret. We believe they've been tasked with killing you and finding whatever information it is you have that their boss wants."

"And who do you believe their boss is?" Sebastian knew who he thought was behind it all, but he wanted to know what they knew and what they wanted from him.

"Before I reveal that, I think it's only fair I come clean about a few things."

Sebastian thought for a moment as the dread he felt earlier came flooding back that perhaps this was how defendants felt waiting for him to pass judgement. A sense of not knowing and having no control over the next few minutes of their lives and like them he thought perhaps he had nobody but himself to blame. "Some honesty would be a novel idea."

Reaper raised a warning eyebrow, but he ignored him. As far as he was concerned this was between him and Snow and nobody else.

"My name is Sabine Goubert and I work for a company called Shadow Elite. As I explained, we're not an illegal vigilante group, we have the highest clearance in the land."

"How come nobody has ever heard of you? Not even a whisper." Even secret groups had stories told about them.

"Because we don't want anyone to know about us and we're good at what we do. If people knew, we wouldn't be as effective. As far as the outside world knows, we're either dead from our pasts or missing. Or for some like Bein, the image of a life lived away from the one he should have had. We keep our real names, but our history is wiped from existence. If you Google us, you won't find anything, not even a school picture."

Sebastian could respect that, understand it even, but that didn't explain their interest in him. *Unless.* "Bein. I recognise him. He's Bram McCullum from the shoot-out with Doyle." He leaned forward; his anger forgotten in his quest for the truth now. "Is that why you're interested in me, because of the enquiry I'm heading up?"

"Your name came up during that, but our interest comes from my own personal reasons."

Now he was intrigued, watching her face as her expression closed revealing nothing to him at all. "And what could your personal interest be in me, Snow?"

"My birth mother is Dominique Dupont."

She said no more, and he rocked back as if struck, the sudden resemblance striking. But how? Nobody had ever heard a whisper of Dominique having a daughter, especially one as beautiful as Snow. The need to deny her words struck him and he stood, pacing to the door and back before he sat once more as another, heftier, realisation struck him. He looked up sharply at Snow and saw she knew he knew and was waiting for his reaction.

"That means you're Fleur's aunt!"

"Yes."

His initial reaction was relief that he no longer had to do this alone. That he had someone who'd love Fleur as much as he did if something bad happened. Despite all the crazy revelations, he knew from watching them together that what she had with Fleur was real. As his brain processed that, hot betrayal that she'd lied her way into his home burned through him. "Why didn't you just tell me?"

Snow had the good grace to look contrite and he could have let her off, but he was angry.

"Great plan. Oh hi, Sebastian. I'm the sister of the man you hate. Can I just get to know my niece? You would've shut me down and rightly so. You're protecting her, I get that."

Now he felt contrite because Snow was right. He'd have absolutely shut her down and taken out every restraining order he could to stop her from getting close to Fleur. "So, you posed as a nanny to get to know Fleur."

"Partly, but also because we needed to know more about your relationship with Dominique."

"Why does that matter to you?"

Sebastian leaned forward, her scent catching him and making his dick stir. Even in this fucked up situation he wanted her, and it was infuriating. That fuck nugget sitting next to her just made it worse by angling his body close to her in an attempt to wind him up.

"Dominique didn't raise me. I've seen her in person once in my life and that was the night she had my father murdered. She let him raise me and turned her back on us because he wasn't the calibre of man she wanted, and by association, neither was I."

Sebastian felt his hatred of the Dupont family double at her words. Acid burned his gut at the thought of the pain and rejection Snow must have felt as a child. He itched to go to her to hold her and absorb the pain he knew she was feeling but his stubborn pride stopped him from moving. "I'm sorry."

A humourless snort came from Snow, and he looked up to see the sad acceptance in her eyes.

"It was a long time ago and I had a good, if unconventional, life with my father, but she took that away and now she needs to pay."

Her voice had gone from calm to cold rage that he'd never heard on her. She was the warmest, most positive person he'd ever come across and this side of her didn't sit well with him. The badass Snow he could handle, she was sexy as fuck, but he didn't like this bitter side to her one little bit. "So, what do you want from me?"

Snow cocked her head and then glanced at Reaper, an unspoken conversation happening which made him see red. As he was about to react, Reaper stood and left the room, leaving just the two of them. Without thought, he stood and went to sit beside her on the couch. Her closeness instantly made him feel better in the strange world he found himself. Sebastian didn't touch her, but he was close enough to feel her warmth as she turned to him.

"You have a history with them. You seemed close to Dominique."

His lip curled and he swallowed the snarl that almost left his lips. "That woman is fucking poison and so is her son."

Her soft hand on his arm made him look at the contrast between her pale skin and his tanner one. She was trying to offer him comfort in this nightmare, and for the first time in a long he took the comfort she offered. Twisting his arm and linking his fingers with hers, the silky texture of her palm so small in his and so right.

"My sister was like you in that she saw beauty everywhere. She believed people and took them at face value. I hated Patrick from the first time I met him and when I looked into him, what I found didn't make me feel any better. He was a narcissistic asshole, bordering on psychotic, and left destruction wherever he went. I tried to warn her but she was in love or so she thought. Then she got pregnant. I knew I had to support her and him or I'd lose her and she'd be alone. I agreed to go and meet his family and spend the weekend with them."

He looked at her as if really seeing her for the first time and saw not only the warmth but now the strength and resolve. She was kind and sweet with a backbone of steel and he was enchanted with all of it.

"Have you ever spent time with someone and know, despite the persona of perfection they present to the world, that inside they're rotten to the core?"

Snow nodded. "Yes."

"That was how I felt the entire time I was there. Like a putrid scum was leeching into me from the rot they were trying to hide. It was clear that Dominique was behind everything her son did, and if not the details, she was certainly the puppet master. Her husband was the most insignificant man I've ever met. He was hardly around and seemed to shrink when Dominique and Patrick were there."

"Yes, Jean-Claude Dupont is a weak man, but he has money, and his family history goes back generations. Which is why Dominique chose him. He's the perfect foil for her political aspirations and that's proven by the seat she holds now."

Sebastian nodded, agreeing.

Snow squeezed his hand. "What happened to your sister?"

His gut roiled at the prospect of revealing the family secrets, but he felt the need to be honest with Snow.

"Lucinda is adopted. It was a closed adoption, and she had no idea who her parents were. After Patrick decided he didn't want to be with her any longer, when the shiny toy of something new beckoned, he told her he wanted her to get rid of Fleur."

Snow winced and ran her thumb over his wrist, feeling the thrum of his pulse.

"Lucinda wouldn't hear of it, so Patrick told her he'd found out that his father was her biological father and that she'd been fucking her half-brother. My sister was devastated and fell into a deep depression. I was worried sick, but she came through it. I convinced her to get some help."

Sebastian pursed his lips. "Lucinda always suffered with her mental health. She had bipolar and clinical depression. She was fine after she had Fleur and was a wonderful mother but after a while, I could see she was off her medications again. She started talking about how she was dirty and sick, how she'd committed the ultimate sin and had a child with her brother. It was all bullshit, but she just wouldn't have it. I had her committed to a psychiatric facility and my mother and I cared for Fleur until she was better."

"That explains why Fleur is so close to you."

"I was there from the start. I was the person she walked to first. I got her her first pair of shoes. Lucinda was getting better and even planning on moving close to me so she could care for Fleur on her own. Then our mother died and she went downhill. Started drinking, went off her meds, and hung herself."

Snow released his hand, and he felt the loss instantly before she leaned forward and wrapped her arms around his neck and hugged him tightly. Sebastian stiffened, his body tensing at the unfamiliar feel before he relaxed his body and returned the hug, wrapping his arms around her small waist. He wasn't a hugger by nature, showing his feelings with anyone but Fleur was unusual for him. It involved him letting his guard down and that wasn't something he did often. Yet he couldn't seem to keep that guard up and in place with Snow. It was as if, from the moment she walked into his life, she'd been breaking down his barriers. He'd fought to keep them up until he didn't know what to think or feel or do.

Tears swam in her eyes, and he lifted a hand to thumb the offending wetness away. He didn't want her to cry for him, he never wanted to be the reason she was sad, and that realisation struck him like a tonne of bricks to the heart. "Don't cry for me."

Snow wiped the rest of the tears away with the back of her hand. "It's not just you. I'm sad for Fleur. That she'll never know her mother and for Lucinda for not getting the chance to raise that beautiful child." Snow looked down and when she glanced back up, he drew in a breath at the absolute beauty of the fire in her eyes and the passion. "And I'm so flipping angry at Dominique and Patrick for what they did to your family."

"I'm sorry they took your dad away from you."

Snow shrugged as if she was over the pain of it, but even after knowing her for such a short time, he knew she hurt way more than she let on. Her sunny personality was real, but she also used it to hide her pain. "I have my team, who are like family to me."

They were still wrapped in some weird shroud of honesty and emotion, her arms now resting on his biceps.

"I hate that you could have got hurt because of me last night." It had weighed on him all night. In his head, he replayed the images of her facing bullets as he walked away. His conscious mind knew he had no other choice, but it didn't help the guilt. He was a protector by nature so letting this scrap of a woman, no matter how well trained or deadly, stand between him and danger would never sit well.

"I'm good at what I do, Sebastian."

"I don't doubt that, but don't fucking do it again."

"I can't promise that."

He could feel her pulling away and hated it but didn't know how to stop her without taking back what he'd said. "And I can't promise I won't do whatever it takes to stop you."

"Seems like a problem for another day to me, so stop being a stubborn fudge donkey."

Sebastian smirked. "Did you just call me a fudge donkey?"

Snow shrugged, her button nose twitching, making his dick harden. How was it that he found that simple move from her more arousing than a seductive lap dance from any other person?

"You were acting like one."

"Can you physically not swear?"

He found the idea that this woman, who was the ultimate contradiction, couldn't let a single swear word past her lips. It made him want to make her lose control. The thought of the word fuck coming out of her mouth made him ache to make her scream it in his ear as he fucked her.

Snow raised her head in a haughty flick. "I can. I choose not to."

"We'll see."

"Snow!"

Sebastian tensed, his hand on her thigh clamping down in an act of possession as Reaper walked into the room.

Snow made no move to get away but looked up with a smile for the arrogant Aussie. "What's up?"

"It's time to go. We just got word that those two idiots you shot last night were working for Patrick Dupont."

Sebastian's jaw went rock hard at the name and confirmation of who was behind the attacks. The desire to rain hellfire down on the evil man who'd destroyed his family flowed through his veins. He tamped all that down to concentrate on the immediate fact that Snow was going somewhere. "Go?"

Sebastian turned to Reaper, who was watching them, hands in the pockets of his jeans, his posture relaxed like a predator ready to pounce and an intently controlled expression on his face that Sebastian couldn't read. "Snow isn't going anywhere without me."

He'd had no idea he was about to make the forward and telling declaration, but it was out, and he realised he meant every word. Instead of taking up the bait though, Reaper smiled wide.

"Good because you and Fleur are coming too." With that Reaper walked away yelling, "Five minutes and we're out the door, baby girl."

One thing was for sure, much more time with him and Reaper in a controlled space and the fireworks wouldn't be the only thing flying, it would be fists and blood.

CHAPTER 15

"I know it seems strange, but the blindfold is for your own protection." Snow had been expecting an argument from Sebastian regarding their retreat to Shadow's headquarters, but he'd been surprisingly amenable. That he loved Fleur so much, along with the heart breaking revelations about his sister, had changed her view of the man completely. Not changing exactly, rather confirming her growing hypothesis that he was indeed a good person with a complex past.

"It's fine, let's just get this done."

Snow leaned in and slid the bag over Sebastian's head so he was unable to see. Fleur was out cold so there was no need to do the same to her. Plus, it would scare her, and Snow drew the line at that.

All the Shadow Elite operatives lived in the underground bunker that was nestled under the earth and rock of the Brecon Beacons, Black Mountains. It was the perfect location and, with the cover of being the mountain rescue team, which they did indeed do on occasion, it gave them freedom and a reason to be there.

The village was small, but the locals had accepted them into the small close-knit community with kindness, most of which could be attributed to the fact the local landlord was ex-SAS and good friends with Jack Granger, the man who'd put this team together and in one way or another saved each and every one of them.

Bein took Fleur in his arms as the vehicle stopped outside the Mountain Rescue Centre, which led to the bunker, although 'bunker' was the wrong description. It was more like an underground luxury complex. None of the team wanted for anything in the apartments in which they lived.

Snow took Sebastian's arm and gently steered him into the building, nodding at Lotus who was manning the desk, and to the back where the lift was situated. When the four of them were inside, Reaper hit the button to send them down. She was mildly miffed with her friend for continuing to wind Sebastian up when it was unnecessary and immature, but she knew her getting involved and fighting Sebastian's battles wouldn't go down well.

The doors to the lower level opened and she stepped into the space, the sense of coming home she usually got wasn't as strong as it had been in previous times.

"You can take the hood off now."

Sebastian reached up and pulled the hood off his head and blinked twice, his eyes adjusting to the bright light, his hair a sexy mess, which made her want to run her hands through it and see if it was as soft as she'd previously thought.

Bás, who she hadn't seen until that second, stepped forward, his hand outstretched in welcome. "Judge Alexander, a pleasure to meet you."

Sebastian shook it, his eyes moving around the space taking it all in and making his assessments. "You too, I think."

Bás chuckled, a deep melodic sound that hinted at the Irish from his childhood. "I'm sure this is all a lot to process. Snow will show you to your quarters and help you get settled and then we can eat and talk."

Sebastian nodded and reached for Fleur, who was waking up and rubbing her eyes. The little girl had been a champ throughout this entire thing but now she was getting justifiably irritable. She curled into her uncle and Snow thought her ovaries might explode from the adorable sight.

As Bás, Reaper, and Bein moved towards Bás' office, Snow led Sebastian and Fleur the other way to the living quarters. The rooms next to her own were free so Valentina, who'd taken on the role of logistics as well as dog whisperer, had said they were all set up ready.

"This is you. There's a keypad alarm on the door so you have complete privacy."

"Does anyone other than me have access?"

"Watchdog and Bás but they won't impinge on your privacy. There are cameras in all the main hallways and communal areas. A gym and living space with a full kitchen are in that direction. Just follow the noise. Any doors that are locked are that way for a reason so please understand that. If you want to go out at any point, ask anyone you see and they'll help you."

Snow knew she was babbling, which was unlike her, so she stepped inside, mentally zipping her mouth. Sebastian was a large, dominant presence behind her as she showed him the two bedrooms, one for him and one for Fleur, which she noted Valentina had put pink unicorn bedding on and added a few toys and games. Snow wanted to kiss the woman for her thoughtfulness and determined she'd make her some of the chilli jam she loved as soon as she got the chance.

"Uncy Seb, it's a unicorn!" Fleur wriggled to get free, and Sebastian set her down as she rushed toward the bed and jumped, hugging the soft toy as she landed.

Sebastian glanced at her with a twitch of his sexy mouth, showing her the dimple in his almost bearded cheek that made her weak in the knees.

"I see that, munchkin."

As Fleur raced around the room looking at the different toys, Snow led the way back out to show Sebastian his room. It was comfortable with a big king-sized bed, thick quilt, nightstands, drawers for his clothes, and a wall with a life-sized waterfall mural on it.

"I know it's probably not what you like, but it's not forever."

"It's fine. It's actually a pretty cool place and you wouldn't know it was underground with all the light."

Snow nodded, feeling awkward, the sexual tension high from earlier in the garden and she could sense the ripples of desire coming from him as he looked at her with hunger.

Sebastian stepped forward and her pulse kicked up in her neck, as she stood her ground.

"You have that look in your eyes again."

Snow's eyes snapped to him, his eyes dark and predatory, the bulge in his jeans making her breath hitch. He was hard for her, the need she felt for him reflected in his body. "What look?"

"The one that makes me want to spread you on that bed and eat your pussy until you scream my name."

"I don't look like that."

Sebastian angled his head as if he was trying to figure out an exceptionally complex math equation. "Why do you lie to yourself and me? Since I hit puberty, women have thrown themselves at me to the point it's been a constant irritation, yet you deny us both what we want."

"And what is it you think I want?"

"My cock in your tight pussy, my hands on your silky soft skin."

Snow could deny that but they both knew it to be a lie. "I do want that, but I also want respect and love and someone to share my life with, someone who's on my side no matter what. Who looks at me as if I'm the only person on earth who matters to him, and that man isn't you."

Sebastian seemed to pale at her blunt and brutally honest response, and Snow knew she was doing the right thing to stay away from him. A few hours of wild magical sex might sate her lust for this man, but it would mean heartbreak and disappointment when he rejected her, and she'd had too much of that to risk more.

"Look, Sebastian, I won't say it's not tempting but we have Fleur to think about and potentially a lifetime of being in each other's lives. I don't want that to be awkward because we had sex and blurred the lines."

Sebastian stepped back, his hands moving to his pockets as he nodded. "You're right. I apologise."

Snow laughed. "Honestly, it's fine. Now, I have a few things to do. Feel free to explore, the fridge in here is fully stocked but if you want anything specific then ask and we'll get it for you."

"Thank you."

Sebastian walked her to the door, and she stopped and turned, wishing things were different and knowing he wasn't the man for her, even if she wished he was. "As soon as we have a plan or any information, we'll let you know."

"I appreciate that."

Snow hid the grin at his stoic response, the cool man she'd met back in place where he belonged. Guarding the gates of his heart, the way she probably should be.

"THAT'S IT, Snow. Use your size to your advantage."

Hurricane was shouting from the floor of the gym as she moved into Bein with a quick move, wrapping her arm around his waist and using her low centre of gravity to throw the huge man over her hip. He landed on the floor of the boxing ring with ease before jumping back to his feet with a grin on his face.

"Oh, it's on now, Snowflake."

Snow grinned wide, the endorphins and camaraderie of sparring with her friends taking the edge off her low mood the last few days. She'd taken care to keep some space between her and Sebastian to let the dust settle between them. She hadn't avoided him as such, but she'd kept their interactions to public places that involved others.

Fleur was in love with the dogs and Valentina had been teaching the bright child a few commands to make them sit and lie down. Fleur now declared she was going to be a vet when she grew up. Sebastian had been working with Watchdog to uncover as much as they could about Lucinda's birth parents as well as going through the information on the Doyle corruption case. Thankfully, that had been used as the excuse for why he was in hiding and was now working remotely for his family's safety. A report of the kind he was doing often led to a lot of media speculation, especially when it involved judges, politicians, and the rich and famous.

Bein lunged with a right jab and caught her in the arm before she could dodge quick enough, the jolt waking her up but not hurting— at least too much. The men here didn't pull their punches in training, the combatants they faced sure as hell wouldn't, so the women of Shadow had to be twice as good as the men and this allowed them to train for it. While they didn't pull their punches in training, they certainly didn't go as hard as they would in the real world.

"What was that, Bein? You a pussy now you're in love?"

Bein raised his eyebrows as Hurricane continued to shout advice from the side-lines. "Oh, now you're in trouble, little girl."

As she'd known he would, Bein came at her hard, his left, right jab combo one of his favourites. Knowing this, she side-stepped and hefted a side kick to the abdomen. Bein let out an oof of air but instead of going down like she expected, he swept his free leg out and took her down to the mat, pinning her with his weight.

This was always a tricky move for her because she had to fight his weight with her slight build. As Bein straddled her hips and she wriggled enough to get one knee between them, her supple body a gift she was always thankful for. Wrapping that leg around the outside of his neck, she used her body to push up and switch out their positions, locking his arm behind him as he faced the floor.

"Wanna tap out, big boy?"

"Snow, you beating my man up again?"

She looked up into the smiling face of Aoife, Bein's soon to be wife and her friend. "He deserves it."

Snow jumped up and as she did saw Sebastian watching her from the side of the room, an intent, purposeful look on his face. Snow cursed her traitorous heart and body as it reacted to the annoying, stubborn, handsome, sexy asshole.

Bein went to greet his lover and Snow began pulling the small sparring gloves from her hands. A looming dominance fell over her and she ignored it, willing her body not to react.

"A word."

Before she could respond, Sebastian had her by the arm and was practically dragging her from the gym and down the hallway.

"What the hell are you doing?"

"Stop talking, Snow."

His voice was a low growl that set her body on fire, but she wisely did as he said, not wishing to start a fight in the middle of the corridor with all the eyes on them.

When he got to his rooms, he kept going until he was outside her door. "Open the door."

Snow did as he said, ready to give this alpha asshole a piece of her mind the second they got inside. He'd crossed the line now and he was going to have it with both barrels.

CHAPTER 16

SEEING RED HAD NEVER MADE ANY SENSE TO HIM UNTIL HE'D SEEN SNOW rolling on the floor with Bein after he'd punched her in the arm. The rational side of his brain knew he was being completely ridiculous. She was a grown woman who could clearly handle herself. So much so that watching her train the last four days of his stay had become a compulsion and a torture.

To say Snow was sexy as fuck when she was all badass and dangerous was an understatement. She was like walking dynamite and if the amount of times he'd had to walk away to relieve the ache in his dick by jerking off like a teenage boy was an indication, he was clearly fucked.

Slamming the door to her apartment closed, he didn't take the time to look around, his eyes had one focus and that was the sexy minx in front of him. Her chest heaved with anger, her cheeks pink and eyes flushed as she placed her hands on her hips and glared at him. His cock was so hard now it felt like it might split his jeans in two.

He prowled toward her, his lips fighting a smirk when she faced him, not moving an inch to back down from his furious glare. She

120

was a feisty little package of contradictions, and he couldn't get her out of his head. Her little speech the other day had made complete sense. She was right, they had Fleur to think of, a child who needed and loved them both and one he knew Snow adored. Her attention to the child hadn't wavered in the slightest since being back amongst her friends and doing her day job—whatever the hell that included.

"I don't know what your game is, Snow, but teasing me by rolling around with other men won't work." Lies, such lies he was spouting.

Snow frowned. "Did you get dropped on your head as a baby? Because let me tell you, nothing I do is about you."

That stung more than he liked to admit. At least it would have if he didn't know she was lying. He could see the outline of her hard nipples through the tight sports bra type top she wore with her tiny shorts. His mouth salivated with the desperate need to flick his tongue over one of those tight buds and make her squirm.

"Liar."

Before she could respond, he had her pinned against the wall, her body held by his as he wedged his knee between her legs, one hand pinning her wrists to the wall behind her. The heat of her pussy against his leg made him groan before he dropped his head and kissed her. Her mouth dropped open in surprise and Sebastian took full advantage, spearing his tongue into her mouth and tasting her desire. Snow kissed him back with none of the hesitancy he might have expected. No, this woman was passion personified and could give as good as she got.

The little moans she made only fuelled the dark desire in his body, which had won the hard-fought battle for control. "Fuck, I need to fuck you, baby."

Her body writhed against his leg with abandon as if they'd both let the leash off their desire and now it had taken on a life of its own.

Snow tore her mouth away and Sebastian begged to a God he no longer believed in that she wasn't about to put the brakes on this.

"I want to feel you inside me, Seb."

"Thank fuck."

Lifting her so her legs wound around his hips, he stumbled to the couch, not having the capacity to make it to the bed only a few more feet away. His lips found hers as they tore at clothes, the sound of buttons hitting the floor melding with the sound of fabric ripping.

Her hand reached for his cock as he lay her back on the couch so he could take in the beauty of her perfect body. No, not perfect in the normal sense. A huge, puckered scar on her abdomen caught his eyes and he reached to touch it before she tried to cover it.

"Does it hurt?" A swell of tenderness and protectiveness for her was almost overwhelming as he brushed her fingers aside and tenderly leaned in to kiss the healed skin.

"No, it's fine."

He could see she didn't want to talk about it, so he swirled his tongue around the nipple of a pert breast that was begging for his mouth. His lips sealed around the tight bud, pulling and sucking as she bucked beneath him, her back arching as she moaned into him, her hand on the back of his head, holding him to her. Sebastian felt a connection to this woman that he'd never experienced before, and it should've had him running for the hills, but he didn't have it in him to walk away from her. Not now, and he wasn't sure if he ever would.

Running his hands down her body he lifted her, his hands under her ass, squeezing the gorgeous flesh as his aching cock begged for mercy. Letting her nipple go as she moaned, he did the same to the other side, his face wreathed in pleasure at the sight of his marks on her pale skin.

He'd never been a caveman intent on marking his territory. In fact, he'd always been in complete control with his sexual encounters but not now. This woman did something to him, and he would've given her anything in that moment and it should terrify him, but he trusted her. A woman who'd lied to him from the start, had kept secrets, still kept secrets but he trusted her in a way he couldn't express or explain.

Looking between them, he saw the glistening pink of her sex, his aching dick stroking through her pussy, rubbing against her clit as they both watched, Snow propped up on her elbows, him on his knees on the floor.

"So fucking perfect."

He kept going, slow deliberate strokes, but no penetration as she got wetter against him until he could smell her desire thick in the air. It was the best thing he'd ever smelled as she moaned louder, her breath coming in little pants as her climax rose.

Her fingers toyed with her nipples as he watched, the confident display making his balls draw up as he tried to recite football scores to stop his orgasm exploding from him and covering her sweet cunt with his seed.

A guttural cry tore from her as she came, her climax something so beautiful he knew he was ruined for other women. As she came down, her body losing the tension, Sebastian slipped a condom over his cock and aligned with her entrance before thrusting inside. There was no hesitation or doubt in his mind as the feel of her exquisite pussy enclosed his cock.

Sebastian held her hips in his hands as he thrust hard and deep, his pelvis rubbing her already sensitive clit with each thrust. Her hips tilted up further and he sank deeper, making them moan as he hit that place deep inside her, his cock rubbing her g-spot.

Her short nails dug into his forearms as she held on, rocking back against him, her eyes lifting so he could drown in the unbridled desire there. She hid nothing, it was raw and real and the best sex of his life.

"You feel amazing, like fucking heaven."

"Seb."

The rest of what she was going to say was cut off as he shifted position, pulling out and flipping her on her belly on the couch as he admired every beautiful inch of her body. "On your knees, baby."

Grasping his hard dick, he gripped tight at the slight curve of her spine and the sexy ass that had driven him so crazy the last few weeks. Driving his cock into her deep, he groaned at the feel of her squeezing him at this angle, her body primed as she held on to the back of the couch and watched him over her shoulder. Her hair whipped around her face, her pouty lips red from his kiss.

His hand stroked up her spine before it tunnelled into her hair, and he pulled, lifting her up with enough tension to sting but not hurt her. As her pussy clenched and more wetness flooded his cock, he smiled a feral aggressive expression of dominance and possession. "You're mine, Snow. Do you understand?"

He wasn't sure what he was saying or doing, only that it felt right.

Snow didn't answer and he tightened his grip, his hips flexing faster as he fucked her harder, deeper. "Do. You. Understand?"

"Yes, but that goes both ways."

Even now, when her hot body was tightening around his cock so hard he thought he might pass out from the pleasure, she was fighting him and he fucking loved it. "Yeah, baby, it does."

Lifting up so her back was plastered to his front, he palmed her breasts, pinching the nipples and palming the soft flesh as his body got close. His free hand snaked to her pussy, feeling the slide of his cock moving into her, coating his fingers with her need. Using the pad of his finger, he stroked her clit as he increased the speed of his strokes. Her body tightened around him as she held on, her arms around his neck, making her tits thrust out further.

She was like a dream, so perfect and sweet and a complete vixen in the bedroom, she was everything.

"Sebastian, harder. Fuck me harder."

He smiled as the swear word registered and his arousal peaked, his balls drawing tight as the tingle along his spine warned of his impending climax. "Come, Snow. I need you to come because that dirty mouth makes me want to come inside that hot body of yours."

As if on command her body convulsed, her channel pulsing around him as a cry tore from her lips and she came, taking him with her. His orgasm was so strong he saw stars or flashing lights, his legs giving way as he fell forward taking them both to the couch, his arms wrapped around her warm body.

He would've stayed that way if it wasn't for the condom between them. For the first time in his life, he detested the piece of latex that stopped him from feeling the pleasure of bathing her pussy with his seed, of skin on skin.

"I need to get rid of this condom."

Snow lifted her body, moaning as he withdrew but not moving much else. He cleaned up and if he'd been a gentleman, he would've offered her a washcloth to clean up but the thought of her marked by him was too much of a turn on. He was turning into a real-life caveman.

Walking back into the living room he took in his surroundings, the touches of her everywhere and knew it suited her. Snow was still lying on the couch, her body gloriously naked as he lifted her up and draped her over his own naked body, his dick already stirring wanting more.

"I think you killed me."

Sebastian chuckled. "Me? I'm the one who is going to be nursing a groin strain tomorrow."

Snow cuddled against him as she laughed, her breath warm on his chest as he held her close. "Want me to rub it better?"

Again, he found himself smiling as he stroked her soft skin. Remembering the scar, he stilled, his body going tense. "How did you get the scar?" Snow moved to sit up, to pull away but he held her still, his hands gentle as he stopped her from moving. "You don't have to tell me, Snow, but don't run."

Snow settled and was silent for so long he figured she was going to stay quiet on the matter. "I was shot by Jimmy Doyle."

Sebastian tensed. His whole body went cold at the thought of how close he'd come to never knowing this amazing woman, who in a few weeks had changed him in fundamental ways. "What happened?"

"He attacked the castle owned by Bein's family. Aoife, Bein's fiancée is Doyle's daughter. He'd abused her for a long time, and she was running when she found us and fell in love with Bein. When

Doyle found us, he attacked, and in the confusion, I got hit by a stray bullet."

Sebastian kissed her head, feeling more shaken than he cared to admit. "Who killed him?"

Sebastian knew he was dead from the file he had, but not how or the details as they'd been kept vague, which made more sense now.

"Bein did."

"Remind me to thank him."

Silence filled the space between them, but it wasn't uncomfortable, rather it felt right.

"What are we doing, Seb?"

He paused, wanting to order his thoughts before he gave more than he was willing. Yet he found in that second there was nothing he didn't want to give her. "I meant what I said. I want you. I want us to be together. I don't know how that will look but I want to try."

"And Fleur?"

"We go careful. We explain to her in a way she can understand, and she doesn't need to know the details. But I want to be able to kiss you and hold you. I'm fucking addicted, Snow."

"I want that too, but it scares me, Seb. You've given me no indication that you have that in you."

"I know, and before you, I didn't. I still don't know if I'm in a position to make you any long-term promises, but for the first time in my life, I want to try. You changed me, baby."

Snow looked at him through narrowed eyes. "Maybe but if we're doing this you need to stop with the potty mouth."

Seb turned so they were facing each other and hooked her leg over his hip, so he could be closer to her. "Me? I have a potty mouth? I think you'll find it was you screaming *'oh Seb. Fuck me harder, Seb'*."

Snow blushed, the pink adorable on her pale skin and he fell just a tiny bit in love with her in that moment.

The notion shocked him, and he immediately went to reject the idea but stopped. Possessive he could understand, he was a red-blooded male, but he'd never been in love, even with the woman he was meant to marry years ago before she showed her true colours by fucking his father.

Yet the idea of falling in love with Snow didn't terrify him like it had with every other woman. Perhaps because he already trusted her with the person he loved the most or maybe it was just because it was her.

CHAPTER 17

To say the last week had been the best of her life was an understatement. What she had with Seb was beyond what she could've imagined. By day she taught Fleur like she had at home but now she included other things. Watchdog had spent the past day teaching the child how to play games on the laptop he'd loaned her, which was actually Python coding. Fleur had taken to it like she did everything else, with aplomb and excitement.

She spent the nights working on the case or curled up with Sebastian, either watching TV or simply talking. Neither one of them had revealed anything deep but it was simple things like his favourite colour or him telling her about his foray into acting that had ended when he threw up on stage from nerves at age seven.

Snow had told him a little about her life, not the details but how they'd travelled and how lonely it was.

"Earth to Snow."

A balled-up piece of paper landed on her desk where she was going through the known contacts of Dominique Dupont and her family. Snow shook her head, blinking widely out of her thoughts and looked at Watchdog.

He was shaking his head at her and rolling his eyes. "Did you know that male Argonaut octopus can detach their penis and send it swimming after the female to mate with her while he stays put?"

Snow bugged her eyes at Watchdog, who chose the strangest moments to throw random, little-known facts at people. "I didn't, in fact, know that. Now that I do know, I'm not sure how I feel about it."

Watchdog blinked and looked up from his keyboard. "Really? I think it would be awesome."

"That's because you wouldn't have to drag yourself away from your computer terminal to get laid."

"See, perfect."

"You're an odd little man, Watchdog."

The smile he sent her was cheeky and endearing just like he was. The man looked like a Greek god and had the mind of Steven Hawking. Better in fact because Watchdog's IQ was off the charts higher than the esteemed physicist.

"So, you and Sebastian Alexander."

Snow groaned. She'd been waiting for this all week since it had become clear to her team she was involved with Seb. They hadn't made any announcements or anything but neither had they hidden their relationship and around there, surrounded by this lot, it would be futile anyway. "Don't start."

"I'm not. I see the way he looks at you, that's not fake."

Suddenly intrigued by what the boy genius saw she turned to face him fully. "Okay, I'll bite. How does he look at me?"

"Like a starving man who's finally found a juicy steak. Like a man in awe of the person he's holding. Like a man in love."

"No, he doesn't."

Her instant rejection of the idea that Seb was in love with her was purely a self-protective gesture and she knew it.

"Okay."

Watchdog went back to his screen and Snow was left to ponder what he'd said. Was Seb really in love with her and if so, how did she really feel about that? The truth was, she was already half in love with him and she adored Fleur but what if it went wrong? What if her evil mother took them away from her? Loving him and losing him would destroy her and she knew it. Could she stop herself from falling more or was it too late?

The questions ran through her mind the rest of the afternoon and into the evening. She went to meet Valentina in the main kitchen.

It was Valentina's turn to cook, and they were all excited about that. Having a bona fide Italian in the kitchen was like a blessing from the gods. Her meatballs were the stuff dreams were made of, and she was going to learn how to make them so she could widen her repertoire. In return, she'd teach Val how to make her fudge.

"Hey, you ready to cook?"

Valentina was a twin. Her brother Rafe was married to the famous rock star Nix. Their reunion after a long misunderstanding had been a Christmas miracle and a romantic story that made her heart sigh. "Sure am. Put me to work."

Val showed her how to season the meat, adding things Snow would never have even thought to use. Then they stood side by side as they rolled the huge amount of mince mixture into balls for frying.

"How is Fleur getting on with the commands?"

Val smiled and it lit up her whole face. "She's an utter delight and a total natural. Has Sebastian had her IQ tested?"

Snow shook her head as she formed the last ball and set it aside on the lined tray. "I don't think so, why?"

"I think he should. I wouldn't be surprised if she gave Watchdog a run for his money."

"You might be right. I'll talk to him."

"Speaking of her hot uncle, how is that going?"

Snow shrugged one shoulder as she washed her hands, getting the grease off her fingers. "Good."

"Just good?"

"Amazing, phenomenal. He rocks my world. I'm falling for him so fast I feel like I'm going to get whiplash."

Val's eyebrows rose. "Wow, all that from good. He must be a god in the sheets."

Snow couldn't stop the smile as she remembered last night when he'd fucked her over the kitchen counter of her apartment making her come so hard, she thought she might blackout, before doing it again in the shower.

"Yeah."

Val laughed. "If that smile is anything to go by, then that's a hell yes. So why so glum?"

"Watchdog said he thinks Seb is in love with me."

"And? Would that be so bad?"

"Yes, no. I don't know."

Val ushered her into a chair. She was slightly older than Snow at thirty-four to Snow's twenty-six, but she was a good friend and would probably give better advice than anyone else she knew there, except maybe Aoife. But she was in Birmingham at her University placement.

"You know who my mother is and what she did to my father. What if she tries to take them from me too?"

Val frowned and reached a hand to her arm, patting gently. "Snow, do you think she killed Henri to hurt you or because of something he did?"

"I don't know but obviously she hates me. She gave me away, walked away without a backward glance. How unlovable must someone be for their own mother to do that?"

"Snow, that wasn't about how lovable you were. I hope you don't believe that."

"My mother left. My father spent his life running from one con to the next using me as his bait before he left me. And I know that's not his fault before you say it. My dog ran away when I was eight, my best friend from high school left for college and never even bothered to keep in touch. Everyone leaves. That can't be a coincidence, it must be me. I'm the commonality in this equation."

"Bella, no. That's not true. People leave or die, that's part of life. You're not unlovable or to blame for other people. You're kind and beautiful and smart and you love hard. That's why you hurt when they leave but you can't close your heart because of that. If you love him, then let yourself do it freely. Don't go forward with the baggage created by others who aren't worthy of you."

Snow felt the tears burn her eyes as she tried to swallow them down, daring to hope that Val was right and yet frightened to do so.

"Hey, you okay?"

Snow looked up to see Sebastian's concerned gaze as he walked toward them looking like he was ready to slay dragons for her. He was so handsome, and she was so totally screwed because there was no doubt she was hopelessly in love with him.

Forcing a smile and wiping the tears, she stood and went to him, feeling Val watching them.

She slid her arms around his neck, and he wrapped his arms around her waist hugging her to him so she could feel his heat all around her. "I am now."

His lips found hers in a soft kiss before he pulled back and really looked at her, his strong jaw shrouded with a soft beard, which felt amazing on her skin. He'd gone to shave last night, and she'd stopped him, telling him how much she loved it, which was how the shower sex had happened. "You busy?"

"Not now. Why, what do you need?"

An animalistic glint in his eye made her shiver as his eyes dropped to her lips again. "Um, I want that too, but unfortunately Fleur wants to show you what Lotus taught her in self-defence class today."

This time the smile was genuine. "Then let's put the first dirty thoughts you had on hold until later and go see our girl."

As he held her hand as they walked down the corridor toward

the gym, he leaned in, his lips brushing her neck making her throat dry with need. "How do you know my thoughts were dirty?"

"Oh, I know, because I'm a very good judge of character and you, Judge Alexander, have a filthy mind."

Sebastian pulled her closer and kissed her neck, a playful side to him she hadn't expected emerging since the walls had come down between them. "And you, Ms Goubert, love it."

Her breath hitched at his words, and he stopped suddenly as if realising what he'd said before he laughed it off and pulled her through the door of the gym. Fleur instantly pounced, running toward them full speed, and landing in her uncle's arms.

"Snow, I can do an X-block. Watch."

She wriggled until Seb put her down and grabbed their hands to drag them closer to the ring where Lotus and Reaper were waiting. Lotus bent and helped Fleur into the ring, where she proceeded to show off her blocking skills as well as a few kicks that Reaper had taught her.

Snow whooped and hollered like a pro, proud of the child who took on life with such courage and enthusiasm. She was like that or at least she had been until the looming threat of Dominique had begun to weigh so heavy.

With every piece of information they dug up on the French President and her family, and most especially that sick son of bitch she called a son, the fear had grown. Now it hung like a putrid un-lanced boil in her life, stealing her joy.

As she watched the smile spread across Sebastian's face at Fleur's antics, she felt her heart squeeze with love for them both. This man who was so stoic and staid on the outside, only showing his soft underbelly to such a few, had let her into his life and shown her what she was missing out on.

His sense of pride and justice was strong, and he wanted to do good in the world through maintaining that system with integrity. The way he protected Fleur and put himself between her and the door when they walked, shielding her when he knew she didn't need it, showed her he cared.

Her watch pinged with a text, and she glanced at it, knowing the tone meant it was an internal communication.

WATCHDOG: TECH ROOM 999

Snow knew that couldn't be anything good and with a heavy dread in her gut went to excuse herself, telling Seb that she had a work thing to do.

He brushed a thumb over her cheek watching intently as if trying to see into her soul and she was afraid if he looked too hard, he might.

Hurrying to the tech room she met up with Bás, Hurricane, and Bein headed the same way.

"Anyone have any idea what this is about?"

Bás shook his head, remaining silent, his stoic expression revealing nothing of how he felt.

"What took so long?"

Watchdog sometimes lost touch with the real world when he was cyber sleuthing and time meant nothing to him.

"We came straight away. What is it?" Snow knew in her gut it was about her.

He pointed at the screen. "This."

Snow looked at the multitude of code running across the screen and had no clue what it meant. She could get by, but this was next level stuff.

"What is it, Watchdog?" Bás' voice was short and terse.

"This is code I caught on the dark web, and it's a hit put out on Fleur and Sebastian Alexander."

Snow felt the blood drain from her face, her body refusing to hold her for a second as the words hit her full force. Bás' hand on her upper arm made her blink and release the breath she'd been holding, getting much-needed oxygen to her brain.

"You good?" Bás showed no outward concern but to those who knew him, it was clear he was worried.

She needed to pull herself together and be the operative they'd trained her to be and not a woman who feared for those she loved. "Yes, I'm fine."

Bás nodded once and let go, his focus back on Watchdog. "Who issued it?"

Watchdog's fingers flew over the keys, his mind working faster than she could imagine as he worked his magic. "I traced it back, which wasn't easy because this asshole bounced around all over the place, but he used a signature I've seen before so I was able to find him through another network."

"Watchdog!" Bás said firmly getting him back on track from his verbal rambling.

"Sorry. So yes, I traced it back to a hacker who goes by Cypher. When I followed the money, it came back to Jean-Claude Dupont."

"Motherfucker!" Bein spat as he paced the room, his fury nothing compared with the cold murderous rage going through Snow's veins.

Bás held up his hand to calm the mood, which was suddenly dark with tension and anger. When someone came at one of the Shadow team, they came at them all and by default because of her, Fleur and Seb were Shadow now, even if they didn't know it.

"Calm down, we need to formulate a plan. Seb and Fleur are safe for now and that's how it will stay."

Bás turned to Watchdog, his hands on his hips as he took control of the room and his operatives, showing the leadership that kept his team operating as it did. "I want everything you can find on Jean-Claude, Dominique, and Patrick. I want to know every person they've ever spoken to, who cuts their hair, who wipes their asses, and then I want to know their connections. We'll meet back here first thing in the morning to form a plan with the new information."

"I don't want Sebastian to know about this."

She knew it was stupid to try and protect him, but this was her fault. She didn't want him to worry when she was going to fix it one way or another, and if that meant her mother's blood on her hands then so be it. She'd slaughter anyone who threatened her family and didn't care what that said about her.

"I'm not sure that's a good call, but it's yours to make for now. If I feel he needs to know then I'll tell him. I know you have something going on with him but this team and those in it are my responsibility, and I have the last word."

"Understood."

"Good. Let's go eat meatballs."

"Ah yeah, my favourite."

Bás put a heavy hand on Watchdog's shoulder. "Not you, buddy. You have work to do, but I'll have someone bring you some."

"Make it an extra big bowl, I need my energy."

"Can't promise that, buddy. You know how it gets when Val makes meatballs."

Snow's lips tipped and she shook her head at her friends. They messed around but they worked damn hard and protected each other. But this fight was personal. She knew the team would have a plan in place, but she'd be gone before they did. She'd seen the guilt on Bein's face every time she winced in pain from being shot saving Aoife, and she wouldn't be able to handle it if something happened to one of them because she'd had the bad luck to be born to such a sick bitch.

CHAPTER 18

SEBASTIAN WATCHED SNOW PUSH THE DELICIOUS MEATBALLS AROUND HER plate with growing concern. He didn't know what had happened, but someone had upset her, and the thought made him want to scour the earth until he found out who and annihilate them. Extreme perhaps but he found Snow brought out all his emotions in extremes, happy, angry, worried, all of it had an intensity where she was concerned.

Laying his hand on her thigh under the table, he squeezed gently to get her attention. She turned tired eyes toward him, her smile, the one he adored, in place but not reaching her eyes.

"You okay?"

"Of course. Just not very hungry."

That was another tip-off. Snow could eat and eat well. She once told him she had the metabolism of a hummingbird, which had to consume its own body weight daily to stay alive.

Sebastian let it go, rubbing his thumb over her inner thigh in a gesture meant to comfort but where they were concerned it was only seconds before he could sense the sexual tension simmering between them. "Wanna get out of here?"

Snow nodded and he lifted Fleur off the long bench seat so she didn't tangle her legs and they said good night to her team, who were so much more than that. Even in the short time he'd been there, he'd felt the bond between them all that moved way past work colleagues.

Bás had tried to explain it was because of how they lived in such isolation, cut off from the world a lot of the time that it was difficult to have normal relationships so the ones they formed were a lifeline. He guessed the secrecy made it that much harder too but hadn't said so.

Sebastian still wasn't entirely sure who they worked for, but he had a strong suspicion given everything he'd seen and heard. He knew that Shadow might not be conventional by any means, but they were essential to the security of the country and their missions, though probably highly grey in tone, weren't carried out with anything other than good intentions and were sanctioned.

He'd also bet every single thing he owned that the government had no idea they existed any more than he had before now. As far as he was concerned that was a good thing as politicians were as bent as any of the crooks he'd sentenced in his courtroom.

Once they'd settled Fleur to sleep as they had every night since they got there, Snow telling her a story and him listening as rapt as his niece, he put the monitor on and took Snow's hand, leading her next door.

He didn't stop in the living area like they usually did but led her straight towards the gorgeous bathroom outfitted with a deep tub with jets on all sides. Letting her hand go, he ran the hot water and added some bubble bath before turning back to her.

"What ya doin' there, judge?"

He cupped her shoulders, her body so delicate under his much larger frame and revelled at the strength inside her. She was the strongest woman he knew and to say he was head over heels in love with her was something that only a few short weeks ago he would've laughed at. Now he knew he'd die for her as she'd been willing to do

138

for him, except hers had been part of her job. For him, it was because he couldn't bear the thought of a world without her. "Just running us a bath. You look like you could do with some pampering."

Snow grinned, her eyes twinkling for the first time since he'd kissed her goodbye that morning and they'd both gone about their days. He'd worked on the report and she'd done whatever it was she did. Fleur had fit in as if this was her home, flitting between them and the others, soaking up all the knowledge she could like a sponge. Snow smiled a lot but the twinkle in her eye was something he recognised now as just for him.

"I look that bad, huh?"

Sebastian frowned, his fingers tightening on her skin. "No, of course not. You're breathtaking as usual but I sensed you were worried about something and clearly you aren't going to divulge what, so I thought I'd try and help you relax."

Her features softened and she reached up her arms going around his neck, so she was flush to his body. "You're a good man, Judge Alexander."

His dick twitched at the formal address, and he squeezed her ass. "If you knew what I was thinking right now you wouldn't think so, Ms Goubert."

Her head tilted to the side. "Oh yeah, and what is that?"

He nibbled her neck, loving the scent and feel of her against him as his dick strained for freedom. "How much I want to fuck you in that bathtub. Rub your clit slowly, tease you until you're begging for release."

Her breath hitched and he felt her body soften into him.

With a sensuous flirty smile, she licked up his neck, making him shiver. "What are you waiting for?"

His body humming with desire, he stripped off her clothes, kissing her body as he did so. When she was gloriously naked, he took her in, his eyes running over every exposed inch of her skin before he stripped off his own clothes.

Testing the water, he added some cold before he lifted her in his arms and stepped into the bath. He settled against the back and held his arms up to her to sit between his legs. The warm scented water, along with the feel of her skin on his, gave him a sense of rightness that he'd never experienced before. He wasn't the guy who took baths or gave a shit about the woman he was fucking, but Snow was more—she was the woman he knew he was in love with.

Using a washcloth he trailed water over her skin, washing her body and hair as Snow grew more languid against him. When her hair was rinsed, he took time discovering her curves, his hands moving over her body. Her pert nipples strained as he tweaked and plucked at them, her body arching against his touch, eager for more.

His other hand snaked down her belly, past her belly button to her bare pussy. Sliding his fingers through her wetness, he closed his eyes in pleasure at the sounds she was making. His thumb moving over her clit in slow circles as two fingers thrust inside her. He knew her body well enough to know it wasn't enough to make her come but enough to drive her crazy with need.

Her breaths were short as she writhed, water sloshing over the side of the tub onto the tiled floor. "Seb."

His teeth nipped her ear as she angled closer, her ass rubbing against his aching cock, which was pressed between them. "What do you need, baby?"

"I need to come."

"How badly?" He increased the speed of his fingers only to slow them when she didn't respond. A moan of frustration left her mouth and he chuckled against her neck, her pulse fluttering wildly. "How badly, Snow?"

"Very fucking badly, Sebastian."

Her aggression was such a fucking turn on, he thought he might blow his load there and then, but he closed his eyes instead, giving her what she needed. Fucking her with his hand until her back bowed and she cried out as her pussy spasmed around his fingers.

When her body began to relax, he withdrew his hand and sucked the sweet taste of her off his fingers as she watched, her hooded eyes pools of satisfaction.

Snow turned, straddling his lap and he thanked God the bath was so big. As she grasped his aching cock and held it at her entrance, he gripped her tiny waist and surged up, his cock impaling her with one stroke making them both gasp in pleasure.

"Fuck, you feel like heaven."

He kissed her and she kissed him back, tongues duelling for dominance. There was a desperation about the lovemaking that peaked at the edges of his mind, but he shoved it away, the sensations she was creating too much. Her body tight and hot around him as she rode him, her hands on her breasts. She was wanton and so fucking sexy it scrambled his mind.

"That's it, baby, ride my cock."

Her movements became uncoordinated as her channel began to pulse, her climax building. Seb was right there with her, hips thrusting into her from below until she shuddered, her body going tight, and his orgasm ripped through him on a roar, his cum spilling inside her body.

As the feelings of intense pleasure eased, he wrapped his arms around her and held her to his body, the realisation that they hadn't used protection surprisingly not bothering him at all. The thought of Snow having his child made him want to fuck her again until that child grew inside her. The primitive notion shocked him but everything about his relationship with Snow shocked him, why should this be any different.

Her body was pliant against him as he lifted them out of the water and deposited them in the shower to wash off before he wrapped her in a towel and carried her to bed.

"I think you broke my body. My limbs don't know how to work."

"Sit and let me dry your hair."

She did as he asked, sitting on the bed as he ran his fingers through her damp hair, the blow dryer warm on her skin. He'd discovered he enjoyed drying her hair and she seemed to love it, her whole body almost purring like a satisfied kitten.

When they were both dry, he pulled the covers off her bed and they crawled in naked. Snow snuggled up to him, her head moving to his chest, her hand resting over his heart as he held her hand in place, their legs tangled. It was intimate and felt natural with her as if he was always meant to hold her this way.

"We didn't use a condom."

"I know, but don't worry, I'm on the pill for my periods and have regular health checks. Although I haven't been with anyone in a good long while."

The thought of her being celibate for a while pleased him. "I'm clean too. I've always used a condom before."

Snow angled her head to see his face, her features hidden in the shadow, but it didn't matter as he could recount every expression by memory. "Really?"

"Really. I never wanted to risk a pregnancy."

"And now?"

He flexed his fingers on her hip, the image of a child with her blonde hair running around with Fleur making him ache for something that up until now he'd never wanted. "Now I find myself wanting lots of things I never wanted before."

Snow didn't respond for a long while and he thought she might have fallen asleep. As his own body began to relax and his mind grew heavy, he thought he heard her say, "I love you, Seb, and I won't let anything happen to you or Fleur."

He wanted to respond but his mind was too far in sleep to speak so he resolved to tell her in the morning.

WAKING HE TURNED, reaching for Snow, who liked to sleep later than he did, which wasn't surprising as he always woke early. The bed was cold and she was gone. Sitting up, the sheet fell from his body. He rubbed his eyes before dragging on sweats and going to find her.

Reaching the kitchen area of Snow's apartment, he discovered the coffee pot was cold and there was no sign of Snow.

Suddenly anxiety built in his body, a sense of foreboding and dread. He dressed quickly and headed out of the apartment to look for her. The corridors were empty, but he knew they would be at this time.

He checked the main kitchen and the gym, thinking she'd gone for a workout but found nobody. On his way back to his apartment, he heard voices coming from the tech room and followed the sound, wondering if perhaps she'd gotten a break in the case and was helping Watchdog.

Stepping inside, the angry faces of Bás, Reaper, and Bein turned to him before a stony look of determination swept over Watchdog, who'd looked up from his screen.

"What's wrong? Where's Snow?" His heart was pumping fast as if he was on a railway track with a freighter heading his way and no way to stop it. He needed to know but he also knew he wasn't going to like the answer.

Bein walked toward him, angling his body as if he'd have to stop Seb from going nuclear. "She's gone."

"Gone? What the fuck do you mean, gone?" His gut twisted with dread and the urge to spank her ass for walking out on them.

"She left at three am. She took all her mission gear and went after the Duponts."

No! His body and mind were screaming at him, trying to deny what he was hearing. "What the hell? Why didn't anyone stop her?"

Reaper stepped forward, his posture angry as Seb stepped up to him, happy to go a couple of rounds with this prick and let some of the tension go. "You were the fucker in her bed. Why didn't you stop her?"

Seb pushed the other man, feeling good when he stepped back and snarled at him. Bein moved between them, his bulk giving no room for either man to get past.

"You're a fucking prick and you've been jealous of me and Snow from day fucking dot."

"Bullshit. What I have with Snow will outlast some stupid fling."

Seb saw red and launched his body forward. "You fucker. Don't you talk about her that way. She's the woman I fucking love and you'll show some fucking respect, or I don't care how hard you think you are, I'll knock your teeth down your pretty-boy face."

"Love? You don't know what love is. A man like you isn't good enough to lick her boots."

"Enough!"

Bás deep voice bellowed so loud Seb wondered if the aftershocks would end with the earth landing on them all.

Bás aimed a glare at him but Seb didn't back down. They might be her family, but he'd go to war with whoever he had to, to protect her.

"Snow found out yesterday that Jean-Claude Dupont has put out a hit on you and Fleur. We think she's gone to try and take care of it on her own."

Seb staggered back, winded by the news and Bein grabbed his arm to steady him as he bent double, his hands on his knees to catch his breath. "Why would she do that?"

Bein looked at him with sympathy and understanding. "Because she loves you and wants to protect you and my guess is she didn't tell us for the same reason. Reaper is going after her now and we won't be far behind."

"I'm going too."

Reaper shook his head. "No way."

Seb's jaw clenched so hard he worried it might snap. "I wasn't fucking asking. I love her and I'm going. I won't have her face those evil fucks alone."

"She won't be alone. She'll have us."

"Yeah, well, she'll have me too, whether you like it or not."

Reaper seemed like he might argue but Bás stepped in and stopped the argument. "You're both going and if I get there and either one of you two has been anything other than an utter delight to the other, I'll bash your fucking heads together. Am I clear?"

Seb remained silent. He didn't answer to this man.

"I said, am I fucking clear?"

"Yes, boss."

"Crystal."

Bás looked between them then nodded. "Reaper, bring him up to speed on the way over and as soon as we find her, we'll let you know where to go."

Seb wasn't a soldier or a badass, but he was a man prepared to do whatever it took for the woman who'd stolen his heart.

CHAPTER 19

Snow watched through the long-range scope as Dominique slid one elegant leg out of the limo, before angling her body with a grace Snow had never seen and stood. She waited a beat as if making sure everyone got a good look at her before she was ushered by her security team into the Hôtel de Matignon, where she was attending a meeting with the French Prime Minister.

As President, she used the beautiful Elysée Palace as her official residence and spent the majority of her time there when she wasn't in the country at her private estate. Snow knew Patrick lived there with her and Jean-Claude but getting to her at the Palace was harder, so she was staking out her offices for a way into the inner circle. All she needed was a few minutes to do what she needed to do.

Leaving Seb that morning while he slept after the night they'd shared had almost torn her in two. The care he given her, the patient understanding and the restraint not to push her for answers even though he knew there was something bothering her, was a testament to how much he cared, and she knew it had been hard for him.

Sebastian may not be a killer like the men of Shadow, but he had the same morals and the same protective nature. He was an alpha and his nature was to fix things for those he cared about, and she knew he cared. He may not have said it, but he'd shown it in innumerable ways.

She tensed as she felt someone lie next to her on the roof of the building that overlooked the Hôtel de Matignon before her body relaxed.

Snow couldn't look at Reaper knowing she'd see the disappointment on his face. "How did you find me?"

"Really?"

Watchdog! "That was quick."

"Yeah, well you know how we are when one of our own decides to be a fucking martyr."

He was angry and, in all honesty, she understood it, but she was trying to keep the only people who'd ever stayed around from getting hurt. "I know you're angry."

"I'm not angry. If you want to see angry, wait until you see Sebastian. That man is fit to be tied."

Snow looked up sharply cricking her neck and wincing from being crouched for so long. "Seb is here?" Her stupid heart raced with excitement or fear, she wasn't sure which, her mouth going dry.

Reaper tipped his head, as he chewed on a cocktail stick, a habit he'd had since he quit smoking and regarded her as if she'd lost her mind. "Did you honestly think he wouldn't come? That man is so far down the rabbit hole with you, he'd walk across hot coals just to see you smile."

"He can't be here, Reap. He isn't trained and there's a fucking hit on him. And who the hell is looking after Fleur?"

"Slow down, baby girl. Seb is secure at the safe house. He isn't trained but he isn't a complete moron either. He's been working with Hurricane to improve his shooting skills and hand to hand combat. You could still take him, but he isn't the newborn babe he was before. Oh, and Fleur is with Valentina, who volunteered to watch her while we haul your ass home."

Snow processed all of that and nodded, then shook her head. "I'm not going home."

"Yeah, we thought you might be a pain in the ass, so the team is heading out now and will meet us in four hours so we can formulate a plan to end this threat against you and your family."

Snow felt tears hit her eyes and tried to blink them away. She wasn't normally so weepy. She was usually the annoying happy one but the last few days she couldn't seem to stop.

"Hey now, save the tears for when Seb spanks your ass."

Snow laughed, snorting inelegantly at Reaper's words which were meant to make her smile and as always, hit the mark. "Is he very angry?"

"Fuck, yeah. I think I saw sparks coming out of his eyes and smoke out of his ears."

Snow chewed her bottom lip considering how this would go and deciding honesty might be the best option. Deciding that she'd done enough surveillance for now and that avoiding Sebastian would only make things worse, she followed Reaper down the fire escape of the tall building and let him drive them to the safe house.

As they got closer, her belly began to flip with nerves. *I'm a badass. I'm a badass* was the mantra she kept repeating to try and stop her hands from shaking. The words were true. She'd been on missions since joining Shadow that seemed like suicide missions, she'd been shot, chased, almost kidnapped, and watched her father murdered, and stolen a priceless work of art from the Vatican that was still hidden in her rooms at the bunker.

As an operative and thief, she was the best. Which reminded her that she hadn't divulged that part of her history to Sebastian. Her being an art thief, and one still talked about in certain circles, wasn't something she just spat out in conversation and Seb was slightly obsessed with the law, being a judge and all.

The car drew to a stop in a quiet part of Paris near the Left Bank, and she looked up at the quaint property. It was usual for the area and in no way looked like the fortress she knew it was inside. It looked ordinary, which was the whole point, to blend in and be forgettable.

Reaper clapped her on the shoulder. "Come on, baby girl, time to face the music."

She nodded and got out of the car, walking behind him as he unlocked the door, hearing the multitude of locks disengage through the steel-reinforced doors.

Inside she was met with silence, and she wasn't sure if that was better or worse.

Knowing the layout from previous stays she headed upstairs where she could hear the sound of someone moving around. Closing her eyes and taking a breath, she smoothed her hair and pushed through the bedroom door.

Sebastian's eyes locked on her as he turned from the window, and she saw relief wash over him before a flicker of anger fought for dominance. He looked exhausted, his eyes had shadows underneath and his hair, which was normally so tidy, was unkempt like he'd been running his fingers through it.

As she tried to form the words to explain and apologise, he was across the room, and she was in his arms. He held her tight to his body as she hugged him back, relief rushing through her at the feeling of home his arms brought to her.

His head bent and she felt his lips against her neck, not in a sexual way but as if he was reassuring himself she was there and safe. She knew she'd been wrong to run now but, in the moment, it had seemed like the right thing to do, and she regretted it.

Seb lifted his head, and she knew he was still fighting the urge to berate her, and she deserved it. "Don't ever fucking run from me again."

"I'm sorry, Seb. I was trying to protect you."

"I know that and a part of me even understands but you're mine, and I protect what's mine, not the other way around."

Snow pushed away slightly to look up at him, his hard body distracting her, and she didn't want to make this worse by pointing out she was the more deadly of the two of them and offend his manhood.

Deciding a change of subject was easier she asked about Fleur. "How is Fleur?"

"I checked in with Valentina and she's fine, loving life as a mini dog trainer. Although I've only been gone a few hours so I'm not sure that's a good indication. Snow, I know this is your job and the truth is, you saved my life back at the house. A fact I relive every night with shame, but I need to know we're at least a team if this is going to work."

"A team I can do." Her smile was almost back to its previous level of sunshine as she grinned at him.

His thumb found her lips and tugged at the bottom one before he hooked his arms around her hips and pulled her close. "There it is. I've missed that smile the last few days."

"I have to say you seem less angry than Reaper suggested you were."

Seb scowled, his forehead crinkling. "Reaper needs to butt out of our business before I shove my fist down his throat."

Snow chuckled. Knowing that the two men needed to work it out on their own, she wasn't getting involved with this for love or money.

At that second her tummy growled. Seb's eyes rose before his normally, or maybe that was formally, stoic expression tilted into a grin. "Hungry, baby?"

"I forgot to eat."

Taking her hand, he towed her down the stairs and into the kitchen, which she knew would be fully stocked by now. Reaper was on his phone and looked at them as they entered, his expression unreadable but she caught the tension in his eyes and wondered what had caused it.

"Everything all right?"

"Yeah, I might have a new assignment coming up."

"Oh?"

Snow waited to see if he'd elaborate but he didn't. She didn't push in case it was because Seb was in the room. Although he was privy to a lot about Shadow now, he didn't know details on anything but her case, and until Bás or Jack Granger said otherwise, it would stay that way.

"Grilled cheese okay?"

Snow nodded.

"That would be lovely, Judge. Thank you," came from Reaper.

Seb shot him the finger and Reaper laughed and got up to make himself a sandwich. That was progress she hadn't expected.

"The team will be here within the hour."

"Oh, I thought you said four."

"Yeah, I did, but they came earlier. Watchdog has some news he wants to share in person."

"That can't be good."

"No, nothing that gets him out of his lair is ever good."

Snow was surprised the news didn't worry her more but having Seb close eased her fear, making her see how silly she'd been to run off like she had. As she ate her grilled cheese and drank the tea Seb had made her, she wondered how she'd ever coped without him in her life, and how she'd cope if this all went wrong and she had to face a future without him in it.

The truth was, she wouldn't and that terrified her.

CHAPTER 20

BEIN, BÁS, WATCHDOG, AND HURRICANE'S ARRIVAL WAS SMOOTH. BEFORE long they were gathered in the back room around a table where Watchdog had set up his systems until it almost resembled mission control back at the base.

"So, now we have everything set up, are you going to share with us what you found that was so important that you leave the protection of your fort and come all the way to Paris?" Snow said it with a smile, but it was to hide the nerves she felt. Ever since they arrived, the tension in Watchdog and the furtive glances he shot her had made her teeth gnash.

"Okay, there's no easy way to say this so I'm just gonna come out and say it. Your father is alive, Snow."

Snow felt her heart stop, the air in the room stilling as if even it couldn't make sense of the words being spoken to her. "No."

She stepped back and came into contact with Seb, who put a reassuring hand on her hip to steady her as if he knew she was about to fly apart.

"I'm sorry, Snow. I should have found it sooner but honestly, I wasn't looking until now, and even then, it was as much luck as anything else."

Swallowing the confusion, she snapped her spine straight. "How?"

"We don't know how but he must've had help to pull it off."

"How do you know it's him?"

Everything in her wanted to deny the truth of this. She'd seen him shot with her own eyes, had grieved for him, buried him, and now they were saying he'd been alive all along.

Watchdog typed some commands on the screen and there he was. The image was grainy and side on. Her father had aged in the years since he'd apparently not died but there was no doubt in her mind it was him.

She felt Seb stiffen behind her, his grip on her waist tightening and she knew he was feeling her pain and reacting to it.

"Where and when was this taken?"

"Three days ago, in London."

"London? What the hell is he doing there?"

Watchdog glanced at Bás, seeming to hit his quota of answers.

"We don't know yet, but we have to assume at this point it has to do with Dominique and you. Could be revenge or a con. We just don't know yet, but we have him now and Watchdog has every program ever invented running looking for his facial signature. If he pokes his head out again, we'll find him."

"Forget it. My father is too good. If you saw him, it's because he wanted to be seen."

Hurricane, the quietest of the group, looked at her. "You think it's a message?"

"I do. I just don't know who for. The only person who might know is Dominique."

"Which leads me to our next conversation. I think we need to draw her out and the best way to do that is you."

"Fine."

"No way."

Snow stepped away from Seb as they spoke at the same time, not wanting his touch to influence anything she did or said next. "Seb, I know you're worried, but Bás is right. If anyone can draw her out it's me."

"Not true, I could draw her out. She'd talk to me, especially if she thought I was here to make trouble for Patrick."

Snow threw up her hands. "Are you forgetting the damn hit on your thick head?"

"No, hang on. This could work."

Snow swung her glare to Bás who just glared back, not the least intimidated by her or anyone else. "What the heck?"

"There's a benefit ball coming up to do with cleaner water and she's attending. What if we get you and Sebastian on the guest list? She won't want to make a scene and the security there will be tight. We can get us in as hotel staff as back up."

"You think she'll just talk to me?"

"No, but if you slip her a phone with a number to contact you regarding Patrick and your father, she'll take the bait. I'm sure of it."

Snow pursed her lips not hating the idea and knowing it probably was her best shot at getting close and finding the answers she desperately needed because so far, all she was collecting was questions. "That could work."

"It will work. Dominique is a control freak, and she won't like knowing you're here without knowing why."

"When's the benefit?"

"Two days from now at the Shangri-La Hotel in Paris."

Snow glanced to Watchdog who was already pulling up the guest list. "Anyone we know attending?"

"Yes, the British Prime Minister and his wife. James Fitzgerald, the Queen's private secretary, and James Colchester, seventeenth Duke of Crossley and chief legal counsel to our Monarch. Oh, and Liam Hayes and his wife Princess Taamira."

Snow smiled despite herself. She adored Princess Taamira.

"Jesus, who the hell are you people?" Seb was frowning as he swept his hands through his hair in agitation. He looked a little shocked by it all and she wasn't surprised. The people they knew and the things they did, didn't always correspond.

She went to answer but he held up a hand. "Forget I asked. I don't want to know. I need a minute. Just get me on that list."

Snow watched Seb leave with worry tinging her belly.

Reaper gripped her shoulder. "It's a lot to take in, give him a minute."

Snow nodded and they got to planning the details of this mission because failure was always in the details, and this needed to be a success.

Keeping busy also stopped her from obsessing over the fact that her father was alive. If she allowed her emotions free rein on that right now, she'd fall apart and that wasn't an option. She needed to deal with the threat to her niece and Sebastian, then figure out how her father's return from the grave made her feel.

Seb came back half an hour later as they were ironing out the details. He looked angry, stressed, and she didn't blame him. This was a damn shit show, and she was partly responsible for bringing it to his door.

"Hey, you okay?"

He nodded but instead of holding her as he usually did or touching her in ways she'd grown used to, he kept his distance. Hurt lanced through her but what could she expect? This was her and something always went wrong. Instead of showing him how much his rejection hurt, she pasted a huge smile on her face and got back to work.

As she lay in bed that night waiting to see if Sebastian would come to bed, she brushed away the tears that wouldn't do her any good. What was it about her that made leaving so easy, that made people want to walk away from her?

Images of her father's death kept replaying in her mind, the shots, the blood, the anguish she'd felt at his loss, and the anger toward the woman who'd done it. Yet all of it was a lie. He wasn't dead. Perhaps the whole thing had been a set-up. That was why the benefit was so important, she needed answers or she'd never rest.

The door to the room she was using clicked open and light from the landing sliced through the room briefly before the door closed, revealing Sebastian's profile. The rustle of clothes being removed made her hold her breath. Her heart raced in a desperate tattoo as she waited to see what he'd do.

The covers lifted, the bed dipping as he lowered his body into it. Snow held perfectly still, her breathing even and deep as if she was sleeping. Relief was sharp, stealing her breath as Sebastian rolled, taking her in his arms and settling her over his body like a blanket, her leg over his hips, her head on his shoulder.

Nestling deeper, she sighed taking in his scent, and the feel of his body making her feel so safe. This man was everything to her and it was scary because if today had shown her anything, it was that if he walked away, she'd be shattered beyond repair.

"I'm sorry, little one."

Snow didn't know how to respond to that. Why was he apologising? Was it for his reaction or for his anger? Snow wasn't sure but she knew this wasn't his fault. He was a pawn, the same as she was for the most part. Both at the mercy of her parents and brother, who it seemed would stop at nothing to hurt each other and damn anyone who got in the way.

Not wanting to go to sleep with this between them, Snow kissed his neck, his beard tickling her skin. Sebastian rolled so he was above her in the shadows, his hard body pressed along her softer one.

His hand stroked her hair away from her face, and although she couldn't see his face, she felt the tenderness in his touch. It was almost reverent, spiritual, the way he touched her, and a sad melancholy seeped through her as his lips brushed hers in a kiss that was meant to be light but as with everything between them, it became an inferno as the spark ignited.

For the first time in her life, Snow knew what it felt like to have a man make love to her. Seb worshipped her body in an unhurried show of connection that ended with them both finding their climax together. As they reached that pinnacle, a tear slipped from her eye because this felt far too much like a goodbye to be anything good.

CHAPTER 21

BEING WITH SNOW THE LAST FEW DAYS HAD BEEN A TORTURE AND A blessing. Since the moment he'd seen the image of the man Snow called father, his world had been spinning out of control as the lies and secrets he'd found himself caught up in finally found him.

Henri Bourdain was alive. Sebastian could definitely attest to that fact. He'd been the man who'd approached Seb not long after Fleur was born with a deal to help him bring down Patrick if he helped him fake his own death. At the time he'd been desperate enough to agree so Sebastian, knowing the seedier people of the world, had set things up. Henri had only wanted his help to disappear and start a new life. Seb hadn't even had to get involved with the details of his death.

Now he was in a hole he couldn't dig his way out of and the worst of it was when she found out, he knew he was going to lose the woman he loved.

As she stepped from the bedroom they'd shared the last two nights, his breath left his body. Her hair was up in some fancy updo with tendrils hanging down her neck, exposing her long, elegant neck and the graceful curve of her shoulders. The dress she wore was the palest gold with tiny straps that led to a deep V that almost went to her midriff. Tiny sequins covered the dress making it seem like it was moving. It moulded her body so not an inch was left to the imagination as it flowed into a long skirt which hit the floor, a side split exposing the creamy skin of her thigh.

He was speechless!

He'd always thought Snow was the most alluring woman he'd ever met but tonight she shone like a star among the clouds.

Moving across the room he took her hands in his and made her twirl slowly, a smile creasing her cheeks at his actions. "You look good enough to eat."

Snow chuckled, her voice warming the places inside him that he'd thought would always be cold and barren. "Why thank you, Judge Alexander."

She didn't wear any adornments and was perfect as she was, having no need for jewels and gems to make her shine more brightly.

Bein stepped into the room, dressed in a tuxedo matching the one Sebastian wore. "Ready to go?"

Snow nodded and bent to adjust the weapon he knew she carried in a thigh holster. The event would be heavily guarded due to the guest list and a security scanner was in use but the weapons they carried could go undetected against any scanner. Just one more thing he'd learned since this adventure into the unknown world of secret assassins and espionage began.

The ride to the hotel was made in silence, with just Snow and Seb in the limo they'd hired. Bein was driving and would make his way inside once he'd dropped Snow and Seb off at the front.

The name of the game was for them to be seen and for the others to go unnoticed. As Bein stopped, Seb could hear the clicks in his ear mic, which was so small he was unsure how he'd ever retrieve the damn thing from his ear. It had taken some getting used to and Reaper, of all people, had been the one to help him get ready for the op tonight.

"You ready?"

He glanced at Snow who he knew was feeling way more anxious than she'd let on and guilt weighed heavy on his heart knowing he'd been involved in part of it, and she still had no idea. "Yep, let's get this done so we can go home."

The way she said home filled him with longing for just that. To have a home with her and Fleur that didn't involve secrets and lies. The truth was, when she found out just how far his betrayal went, she'd never forgive him, and he didn't blame her.

Pushing that thought to the back of his mind, he exited the limo, reaching in to take Snow's hand and help her from the vehicle. The cameras behind them began to flash as he led her up the red-carpet lined drive and past the photographers who were calling his name. As the youngest Judge in history and a wealthy man in his own right, Seb had been around the circuit for a while before Fleur had settled his life into something he hadn't known he'd needed.

Yet it was Snow's attention they wanted. She calmly, and with the grace of a seasoned actress, smiled and ignored them. While they were making waves at the front, the rest of the team were getting into position. Little did these photogs know that the images they were snapping away were already being corrupted as they were taken by the genius that was Watchdog.

Sebastian fully believed that if he chose to, he could very well take over the world during his lunch break. The thought left his mouth dry when he realised that he'd soon find himself on the wrong end of these men who were so dangerous and so protective of Snow.

Inside, the hotel was magnificent in its splendour. He could certainly see why it had been chosen. Making their way through the crowds they headed deeper into the room. He snagged two champagne glasses from a passing waiter. Not that he had any intention of drinking any, he needed his wits about him tonight.

Sebastian had a bad feeling about this entire approach, only fortified by the fact that he couldn't get hold of Henri. He'd tried as soon as he realised who he was and that he was close but got no answer and when he'd tried again later, the number had been disconnected.

"We should mingle."

Sebastian offered his arm as they made their way around the room. He recognised all the people Snow said they knew. James Colchester, who was here with a stunning brunette. James Fitzgerald, who was talking to the minister for education, and then there was Liam Hayes and Princess Taamira.

A more unlikely pair you wouldn't see, but the way they looked at each other was unmistakable and so full of love and desire it was as if no other people were in the room. Seb glanced at Snow, and she was watching them, the same soft look on her face when she looked at him and his heart almost cracked in two to know he'd hurt her.

All of the people who knew Snow ignored her, as there was an unwritten rule not to acknowledge each other in public. Perhaps that was the case or maybe they'd been spoken to beforehand and been told not to react to her.

A slow song came on and he had the urge to dance with her, to hold her as the music played, even knowing it might be his one and only time. "Dance with me?"

Snow startled and he had a feeling she'd been miles away, thinking of who knew what. "Now?"

"Yes."

"But we have to find..."

Sebastian didn't care about Dominique or anyone else at the moment. He pulled her into his body, discarding the full glasses of champagne to a passing server.

"Fine. One dance."

Her lips tipped into the smile he loved, and he moved her around the floor with ease as if they'd been doing this for years. Being with Snow was easy in every way possible, but still exciting. He knew it would always be this way with her, that he'd always experience a thrill of excitement when she walked in a room, tempered with the ease of being with someone who let him be himself.

It was on the tip of his tongue to tell her he loved her, to fall on his sword and spill the putrid truth of his betrayal, however unwittingly, when he caught sight of Dominique Dupont heading towards them. "Heads up. Evil Queen at six o'clock."

He stopped Snow from turning, holding her tighter when she went to move. Reaper was across the room watching as he spoke with a redhead who was hanging on his every word. He couldn't see Bás or Bein but knew they were close.

"Sebastian, how lovely to see you."

The crowd had parted for Dominique like the Red Sea as the dancers moved aside and he could feel every eye in the room on them. "Dominique, nice to see you again." The lie stuck in his throat like glass, but her attention wasn't really on him. It was on Snow who was watching Dominique with barely veiled hatred.

"And who is this lovely young thing?"

He stuck with the script the team had agreed to. "Let's cut the crap, Dominique. You know very well who this is. Now would you like to have this conversation here or somewhere private?"

Snow had remained silent, and he could feel the tension coming off her in waves. After everything his woman had been put through by the people who should have loved her the most, he had the overwhelming urge to step between the two and protect her, even though she didn't need his protection.

Dominique's face remained pleasant at his words, but he caught the slight twitch of her jaw and wondered if she was truly that great an actress or if the Botox just wouldn't permit her to show how she was feeling about this sudden turn of events.

"I don't think there's any need for unpleasantness, Mr Alexander, so why don't we take this to the salon on the second floor where we can have a moment of privacy."

"As you wish."

Sebastian followed, his hand on the small of Snow's rigid back as they ascended the stairs behind Dominique and her guards. There was no sign of Patrick or Jean-Claude but that didn't mean they weren't there, simply that he hadn't seen them. Although he suspected they knew he and Snow were there by now.

The hallway led to a large room that overlooked the back of the hotel, the interior luxurious and tasteful, with two long cream couches facing each other with an antique low table in between. "Please take a seat."

"I'd prefer to stand."

Seb glanced at Snow beside him and itched to take her hand in his but didn't want this woman to know the extent of their relationship. Snow stood tall, her back ramrod straight, neck extended, chin up. She looked powerful, like a force of nature, and nothing like the woman who'd rolled around on the floor building a fort inside his home so they could watch a kid's movie with Fleur.

Dominique's hands fluttered. For the first time since he'd known her, she looked almost nervous but quickly recovered, tucking her hands behind her back. The dark navy sequined gown she wore hid any residual nerves as she straightened her spine.

"I know you hate me, Sabine, but I'd like a chance to explain."

Snow rolled her hand. "Then explain why you murdered my father in cold blood."

"Your father isn't the man you think he is."

"Oh please. Is this where you give me a sob story about how it wasn't you, it was him?"

Dominique was a powerful woman but, in that moment, Sebastian didn't see the President of France, he saw a mother.

Dominique sat on the couch as if her legs were weak suddenly. "No, I'm as much to blame as anyone."

Snow's expression didn't flicker and yet he knew it affected her. He could read the slight changes in her body language.

"When I met your father, I was a young, ambitious woman. He was handsome and charismatic, full of fun and daring and I loved him. As time went on though, I began to see the small manipulations, the way he'd sway me to his thinking without me even being aware. I was about to leave him when I fell pregnant with you. I knew I couldn't raise a child and chase my dreams alone, but I couldn't abort my pregnancy."

Big eyes full of emotion and so much like Snow's looked up at them. "I loved you from the second I found out about you. My pregnancy was easy and when you were born, Henri and I loved you to distraction, but we fought constantly. When you were six months old, I got ready to leave him. I went to the bank and withdrew all my savings. When I returned, he was gone and so were you."

"You expect me to believe that he stole me?"

"Technically it isn't stealing. We had joint custody as he's on your birth certificate. I looked for you for years but eventually, I had to give up or it would've killed me. I met Jean-Claude and despite what people think, he's a good man and we love each other. It's never been the love I shared with Henri, that wild destructive love but it was safe, and we had Patrick."

"Ah yes, my messed up half-sibling."

"Patrick is troubled that's true, but underneath it all, he's a good person. He's just sick."

"Sick! He told my sister they were related, and that Fleur was the product of incest."

"He shouldn't have done that, but he's getting help now. He knew there wasn't any kind of relationship between him and Lucinda other than romantic."

"She fucking killed herself because of it."

"I know and I'm sorry for that."

"What about Henri?"

"What about him?"

Snow stepped forward slightly and he moved with her. He could hear Reaper and Bein in his ear and knew they had eyes on Patrick and Jean-Claude.

"Why did you kill him?"

"Well, we both know it didn't work, but I shot him because he was blackmailing me. He discovered my son was involved with an

Irish mafia leader named Jimmy Doyle and was going to leak it to the news unless I gave him some information."

"You shot him in front of me." Snow's voice broke and he moved closer, lending her his strength without touching her and making her seem weak.

"He said you were away. I never would've done that if I'd known. Despite what you think of me, I never stopped loving you."

"Bullshit. If you loved me, you'd have found a way to get me back."

Dominique looked away, blinking before she composed herself. "I know I can't fix what I broke when I left you with that man, but I'm sorry, Sabine."

"What was the information?"

Dominique looked to him as if remembering he was there for the first time. "I can't tell you that."

Two pops outside the door made them both start. Dominique rose from her chair as the door flew open and the man everyone was talking about strode in, a gun held out in front of him.

Without thinking, Sebastian moved to put Snow behind him but she evaded him, even as he tried to grasp her arm.

"Well, isn't this a nice family reunion?"

"Dad!"

"Hello, button. Did you miss me?"

"Are you kidding me right now? Is that all you have to say to me?"

"You're angry with me. I get that. I did a bad thing, but I had my reasons."

Henri was tall and wiry with grey hair and an angular face. His blue eyes were darker than Snow's and honestly, he could see nothing of the woman he loved in the man. She was her mother through and through.

"Why are you holding a gun on us?"

Henri tipped his head. "Come on, button, you know the score.

Control the room and Seb here looks ready to take me out if I even look at you wrong."

Henri swung his gaze and the weapon to Dominique. "Now this bitch. I'd shoot her for free, but I need some information that she's just not willing to give me. So I'm going to make this interesting."

"Dad, stop."

"Come here, button, or I'll put a bullet in your mother's head. You wouldn't want to see both your parents die in front of you, would you?"

His cruel mouth twisted in a grin that told Sebastian he was enjoying this and didn't care who he hurt.

"Sabine, don't."

Henri fired the bullet hitting Dominique in the arm. She screamed, falling. Seb reached out to catch her before she hit the ground.

"Stop, I'll do what you ask."

"Snow, no!"

Even as he eased Dominique to the couch, he reached for Snow to stop her, but he was too late. She was beside her father who grabbed her, wrapping an arm around her neck. Snow didn't show any emotion but gave him a slight shake of her head.

"That's my girl. Dominique, you have twenty-four hours to give me what I want, or your daughter will be sent back to you in pieces."

"How could you?" Dominique sobbed, holding her arm which was barely a flesh wound.

"Well, I wouldn't do it myself, but I have some interesting friends who'll pay well for a jewel like Sabine."

With that, Henri backed away, his weapon still on Snow. He didn't move towards the door, but towards a bookcase, which turned out to be a hidden passage.

Sebastian was frozen. He saw in Henri's eyes that he meant every word of what he said. He'd kill Snow if he didn't get what he wanted.

As soon as the door closed, he launched himself at it, scrabbling to get it open, but the seams were flawless. The main door burst open and Bein and Bás rushed in, the two men taking in the scene in an instant.

Bás strode toward him. "Which way?"

Sebastian pointed toward the wall and Bás took charge, leaving Seb to feel like the biggest failure in the world. He'd let the woman he loved be kidnapped by a narcissistic asshole and had done nothing to stop him.

CHAPTER 22

S<small>NOW HAD ALWAYS KNOWN HER FATHER HAD AN EDGE TO HIM, HIS TEMPER</small> growing up had been unpredictable at best, but he'd never raised a hand to her in anger and until today she'd never believed he would. Yet, the man who bundled her into the back of a van wasn't the man who'd raised her.

Jumping in behind her, he grabbed a cloth and aimed the gun at her head. "Turn around."

Snow did as he asked, needing time to assess the situation before she reacted. Henri bound her wrists tightly, leaving no room for her to move before pushing her forward so she hit the floor of the van with her face. Pain exploded in her cheek making her blink away the tears, but she didn't give him the satisfaction of crying out.

He bound her ankles as his hands explored her body, making nausea and disgust swim in her belly at the way he was touching her.

He took the gun and her shoes, leaving her feet bare so she couldn't run. "Naughty, naughty, button. Guns are dangerous."

"Get your fucking hands off me."

"Come now, Sabine. It's only me."

"Exactly. You're my father and you shouldn't be touching me that way."

Henri's laugh filled her with fear of the worst kind as his hand touched her inside thigh. "But am I?"

She had no chance to reply to his bizarre comment before she felt the sting of a needle in her neck and her world became fuzzy, before turning black.

When Snow woke, she was on a soft bed. Her body felt heavy with whatever drug her father had given her and her mind was mired with a foggy sensation, making ordering her thoughts a diffi-cult task.

She sat up slowly, sickness swimming in her belly as she tried to swallow past it and take a few deep breaths. Still bound at the ankles and wrists, she saw a light coming from the corner of the room. Henri was sitting in a chair watching her, his fingers steepled in front of him, leg crossed over the opposite knee. He looked relaxed as if this was just another day.

"Good. You're awake." He stood and walked toward her, gripping her chin hard so he could look at her, as she tried to pull away. "I see you're still sulking. No matter."

Gripping her upper arm, he hauled her to her feet, dragging her to the corner of the room, which was bare white walls, no windows and just the bed, a seat, and a lamp. As she stumbled, trying to give the illusion that she was weak and unable to defend herself and buy herself some time, he stopped and turned to her, his face a mask of anger and impatience.

"Stop fucking around, Sabine."

Reaching the corner, she had no idea what he was planning until he pulled her arms over her head and hooked the rope to a hook in the ceiling, her tiptoes just touching the ground. Her shoulder joints stretched, and she was relieved her arms were in front of her instead of behind as they had been when she was first knocked out.

"Why are you doing this?"

Henri walked over to the door, opened it, and grabbed a bucket and a car battery. Through the door, she could make out some steps but little else. Her eyes fell back on the car battery and the bucket, which she could now see contained a sponge and water.

Ice-cold fear crawled up her spine when he brought over a tripod, which had been leaning in the dark corner, and began to set it up. She knew pain, had withstood her share but this was torture meant to get hardened criminals to talk. Her mind went to Sebastian and Fleur, of the time they'd spent together, of the love and fun they'd shared.

"In answer to your question, I'm doing this because Dominique needs to learn that I mean what I say. She thinks I'm bluffing. I'm going to show her I'll do what it takes for the information I need." He moved closer, a blade flickering as he used it to cut her dress from her body, leaving her in just her underwear, what there was of it.

Needing to take her mind off the awful, vulnerable position she was in, she asked another question. "And that is?"

Henri grinned and she could see the madness and greed in his eyes. "The Caribbean Pink."

"The pink diamond that was lost over one hundred years ago?" It was hard to believe he'd go to all this trouble just for a jewel, but then Henri had always been obsessed with jewels. It was why his nickname was Magpie.

"It's not lost. Jean-Claude's family have been hiding it. Dominique is going to give it to me or I'm going to kill you." Bending, he dipped the sponge in the water and used the clip on the jumper cables attached to the battery to pick it up.

As he moved toward her, Snow stilled, not giving him the satisfaction of showing her fear. "You're willing to kill your own child for a diamond?"

Henri shrugged. "Except you aren't mine, Sabine. That's what I was trying to tell you. Dominique is nothing but a lying whore. She cheated on me with Jean-Claude. You're his brat, not mine."

As the shock of the revelation spun in her mind, he touched the sponge to her bare skin and pain unlike anything she'd ever known shot through her. A scream tore from her lips as her body jerked and spasmed uncontrollably.

When he took the sponge and the electric current away, she sagged on the hook, the pain in her arms nothing compared to the rage of fire moving through her body.

"I have to say you're tougher since you joined that team you work with."

"Why did you send Jack to help me if you hate me so much?"

"I don't hate you, Snow. I loved you all your life and I knew if something happened to me you'd need someone to guide you. I saw the jobs you pulled on your own. They were sloppy. I taught you better. I never guessed you working for them would cause me so many problems though."

"How did you know Jack?"

"Well, let's just say his boss has a few nice gems of her own and I got caught. I agreed to flip on other acquaintances if I heard they might target her. We came to an agreement."

He held the sponge to her skin once more and pain was like a red-hot blade through her body.

Breathing deep to get her breath, she lifted her head to see him smiling as he recorded every moment. "Sebastian will kill you for this."

"Ah, Sebastian. The fine upstanding judge." Henri walked around her, moving slowly and she tried not to flinch when he ran a finger along the scar from her bullet wound. "Here's the thing. Sebastian isn't who you think he is. You see, he's been working for me this whole time. He was the one who set up my new identity."

Her whole body rebelled at the words he spoke even as she saw the truth on his face. "You're lying."

"No, ma Cherie, I'm not. Sebastian has been helping me in exchange for the truth about his sister's birth family, which I had delivered to his home address just after you left."

Betrayal and a sense of loss like she'd never known lanced through her, causing an emptiness that left her hollow. No anger, no pain, just a cold nothing that took with it any vestige of her will to live. "Did you send the men to kill Margaret and attack the house?"

Everything was making sense now. She could see the men she'd surrounded herself with and trusted with the most precious part of herself, her heart, were nothing more than vultures out for themselves, willing to pick apart whatever she'd give in an effort to feed their own desires.

"Yes, clever girl. I had to make you think it was Patrick though to throw you off the scent. My girl is too quick for her own good."

"Why did you take me if you hated me so much?"

"There are two things in life that will sustain a person, leverage and the long game."

Snow snorted. "I think the quote reads, health and hope."

"See, adorable, and you not only gave me leverage against a powerful woman but also a cover that was priceless. With you by my side, I was unstoppable. Nobody could see past the adorable child who loved her father. I was untouchable."

"So, it was all a long con then?"

"Yes, but we had some fun, didn't we?"

Snow remained silent for a moment trying to catch her breath from all the things she'd learned in the last hour. "The hit. Was that you?"

Henri chuckled like a child being caught with his hand in the cookie jar. "Guilty."

His watch beeped and it was like seeing a switch being flicked as he turned from one person into another. His face changed, the grin smoothing, the laughter in his eyes leaving, and a coldness came over him. "Time to send the video and let them know they have less than six hours to go."

Snow looked away, not caring what he did. Her body might feel but her mind was in another place now, somewhere safe from everyone who wanted to use her. Her mind went to Fleur, and she wondered if even that had been real. She would've laid money on the fact Sebastian loved her, that his cool exterior was a front for the pain he'd suffered, yet it was all a lie.

Everything was a lie, but she wouldn't die there. No, she wouldn't give anyone the satisfaction. She'd get out of there and go where nobody could hurt her ever again. Shadow would help her set up a new life. Her friends would understand, but even they weren't enough to make her stay in the face of everything else she'd suffered.

CHAPTER 23

Sebastian shoved his hands through his hair in agitation as he paced the hotel room, trying to stop himself from drowning in guilt and to be of use to this team. Dominique was getting her arm stitched but refused to leave the hotel, insisting she was fine. She was tougher than she looked and had a will of steel.

Dismissing her security team to secure her son and husband, she'd shown genuine concern for them.

"Sebastian!"

Seb turned his body toward Bás as he walked toward him intent in every step as Reaper and Bein watched from the other side of the room with open hostility.

"We need to talk."

Seb looked down and he knew it was time for the truth, Snow's life was on the line, and he'd do anything to save her. "I know."

"Let's start with when you met Henri Goubert?"

Seb sat heavily on the arm of a couch, his whole body heavy with fatigue and defeat. "Henri approached me after Lucinda died and offered to help me find the truth of her parentage if I'd help him disappear. He explained he'd been in a relationship with Dominique years ago and knew how poisonous she was and wanted to help." Seb shrugged seeing how naive he'd been now. "At the time I was grieving and all I wanted was the truth so my sister could rest easy, and my niece would never have that black cloud hanging over her head."

"Did you know he had a daughter?"

Seb shook his head. "No, of course not. We weren't friends. It was a business arrangement. I sorted out the new paperwork for him and he disappeared. I thought for a while I'd been scammed but then small titbits of information started arriving and my sister's history began to become clearer."

Bás crossed his arms over his chest. "Did Henri ever mention what he did for a living?"

Seb could understand his anger. Even though Bás was outwardly calm, Seb wouldn't be surprised if he put a bullet in him and he wouldn't blame him either. "No, I guessed he was a criminal but didn't ask questions the less I knew the better."

"Have you ever heard of Bijou Chasseur?"

"Yes, in passing but I've never had a case involving him."

"Them."

Seb frowned not understanding. "Pardon?"

"Bijou Chasseur was a two-person team. They were jewel thieves and probably the best in Europe, stealing millions of pounds in gems and precious metals, also priceless paintings and artefacts. A few years ago they stopped."

Seb had an ache in his gut, and he didn't want to be sitting here and listening to this rubbish. "Get on with it, Bás. We need to concentrate on finding Snow, not you giving me a fucking history lesson."

Bás glanced at Dominique who was speaking to Reaper and Watchdog. "Henri and Snow were Bijou Chasseur. From the day she could walk he trained her to steal, to pick pockets, con people for him. It was a ruse that was often overlooked giving him the perfect cover. For her, it was a fun game she played with her father until it wasn't. She knew no other life, so she stayed and each job they did, a little more of her died. Then she saw her father murdered or so she thought, and when Shadow found her, she was a lost, young woman. But through her own grit and determination she's made herself into one of the best operatives in the field, if not the best, and now she's in danger because of you."

Seb thought he might be sick as his gut churned. He stood quickly, needing air before the information in his head choked him. Pushing past Bás, he rushed to the balcony and sucked in a lungful of the cool night air. He wanted to be angry about the secrets she'd kept from him, the history she hadn't shared but how could he when he'd been keeping his own, and now she was gone.

His mind kept replaying the scene with the four of them in the room and something didn't sit right. He couldn't figure out what it was, just that it was important to finding her. Henri had been angry with Dominique, hateful even, and that was easy to understand but he'd also been resentful of Jean-Claude.

He closed his eyes, seeing the woman who'd stolen his heart in his mind's eye, picturing her face and her smile and then it came to him. Turning from the railing, he rushed back into the room and strode over to Dominique. Grasping her arm, he spun her toward him angrily. "Who is Snow's father and don't fucking lie to me."

Dominique looked away, shame written all over her face.

Reaper stepped between him and Dominique. "What the hell is going on?"

He peered around the furious man, his own fury on a rolling boil, adrenaline pumping through his veins. "Tell him."

"Jean-Claude is her father. We had an affair when I was with Henri. Henri didn't know, but I fear he does now."

Reaper blinked, his normally calm façade evaporating as he rounded on Dominique. "The fuck. You know if he knows, there's no reason for him not to kill her!"

"I know and I'm sorry. I should have told you."

"Damn right you should," Sebastian spat. "What does Henri want from you?"

Dominique shook her head. "I can't tell you."

Sebastian's lip curled in disgust as he stepped forward, Reaper moving aside and letting him take the lead. "You'll tell me, or every single dirty little secret you have will be in tomorrow's paper. Including all the sick shit that pathetic son of yours has done over the years."

Dominique paled, seeing the truth in his words. Her shoulders sagged in defeat, and she reached for a chair behind her to steady herself. "Fine I'll tell you everything, but you need to promise me you'll get my son the help he needs."

"Fine." Seb personally thought a secure mental facility for the rest of his life would work but didn't voice that. He felt the rest of the team move in closer as she began to speak.

"Ever since we met, all Henri talked about was The Caribbean Pink. It's the largest pink diamond in the world and he was obsessed. He'd make plans on how he'd find it when nobody else could and his life would be set. He'd go down in history as the greatest jewel thief of all time. At first, it was fun, but I began to see how it had become a sickness. Then I met Jean-Claude at a charity function I'd attended with my parents. We got on and he was steady, kind, sweet, and safe. Jean-Claude knew about Henri but begged me to marry him. He offered me the life I'd always wanted, so I agreed, and I found out I was pregnant. I honestly thought the baby was Henri's. So I stayed, trying to make it work but he was moody. We fought all the time, but he adored Sabine."

Sebastian watched her face change with the emotions she was feeling as she told the story.

"Anyway, I'd had enough and decided he was too unstable and was going to leave. I met with Jean-Claude, and he agreed to take Sabine in as his own. But I think Henri followed me because he got more controlling and one day he disappeared with Sabine. I looked for them for years, shunning Jean-Claude, until eventually, I knew I had to move on with my life."

Dominique wrung her hands together in her lap and he could see the next part was the bit she didn't want to tell them.

A growl escaped his throat and Reaper chuckled as Dominique flinched. "I think you need to come out and say it, Dominique, before Sebastian forgets his manners."

"Fine. When Jean-Claude and I married he took me to their family Chateau in Cap Ferrat on the French Riviera. There he showed me The Caribbean Pink. His grandfather had stolen it from the Nazis during the war and it was still believed to be lost."

Bein crossed his arms looking fierce. "Wait, how had he stolen it from the Nazis?"

Dominique looked away, her cheeks red before she went on. "His grandfather was a German Spy who turned when it became clear they'd lose. He took what he could and fled home and was hailed a hero. So, you must understand, if this gets out our family name and my position would be destroyed."

"Of course. Who wants a traitor running the country?"

Dominique stood abruptly, thrusting her chin in the air as she faced the five of them down alone. "I'm not a traitor, and neither is my husband. He's a good man, who's shackled by his past as much as the rest of us."

"That may be so, but his past is threatening the woman I love."

Dominique gasped, a smile tilting her lips. "You love her."

Sebastian turned away, not prepared to have that conversation with her, instead concentrating on Watchdog. "We need everything on Jean-Claude's family and any properties they own. Also, check the son's name. Get a list from Dominique of every place they lived as a couple and those that were special to them. Henri will go someplace that means something to them." He glanced at Bás who was smirking. "What?"

Bás spread his hand. "No, please go ahead. Give my team orders. I'll sit over here and take a break."

"You got a better plan?"

"Nope. But I do have a question for the fine President."

"What is it?"

"Why did you dismiss your security before coming up here with Seb and Snow?" Bás angled his head in question and something that hadn't felt important was suddenly imperative. "And why is this place not teaming with police after two of your security details were killed?"

"I wanted privacy."

Bás stood shaking his head. "No, I don't think so. I think you and Henri planned this together. You knew Snow would come and you dismissed your team from the room, leaving only two outside for Henri to deal with. I think you and Henri re-kindled your affair when you helped him fake his death." He walked closer with every step, making her step back. "I think you hate Jean-Claude for landing you with a parasite like Patrick and you wanted some fun. Tell me, Dominique, did you plan to kill Jean-Claude and Patrick, or just Jean-Claude?"

"You know nothing." Her anger cemented her guilt, as did the way she looked at Seb as she spoke.

"Except Henri didn't know until Jean-Claude told him that Sabine wasn't his blood and now you have two men who hate you. Or three if you count the son you were going to betray."

"How do you know?"

"We aren't a bunch of fucking amateurs, Dominique. Watchdog found all the emails."

"I just wanted the excitement back in my life."

"Uh, boss, an email just got sent to Sebastian."

Seb and the others rushed over to Watchdog and a feeling of dread pooled inside him like lead tied to a helium balloon. Watchdog clicked the link and a video started playing, the sound was turned off, but the image was clear. Snow was tied to a hook in a bare room, her feet barely touching the ground, her shoulder joints extended with all her weight on them. Her clothes had been stripped so she was just in a black thong and a lace, strapless bra. Her hair covered her face as it hung low.

The tension in the room was still as they watched Henri walk into shot carrying what looked like jumper cables with a sponge hanging from it, the drips of water falling to the ground. He wanted to look away, not sure he could endure what would happen next but unable to let Snow face this alone even though he knew she already had.

With a smile for the camera, Henri held the sponge to Snow's skin. Her body bowed, contorting in pain as the current from the battery at his feet went through her. Seb didn't need sound to hear her screams, his fingernails cutting into his palm as he clenched his fist to stop himself from punching it through the monitor.

Bein pointed at something to the left of the battery. "Fuck me, is that a car alternator?"

Bás swore viciously. "Yes."

"I don't get it."

"A car battery on its own, even on wet skin, will hurt but not to the degree Hollywood would have you believe. But if you add an alternator, it pumps the amperage up to a degree that's unbelievably painful and oftentimes deadly."

A whimper from behind him had Seb spinning in fury at the woman who'd orchestrated this. "Well, you got your excitement. So tell me where Henri has taken Snow."

"I don't know."

Sebastian pounced, his hand grasping her scrawny throat and squeezing as fear lit her features and he became a man he didn't recognise. "Don't fucking lie." His hand flexed and he knew he'd happily squeeze the life out of this bitch if it meant saving Snow.

"There's a cellar in our first apartment in Montmartre. I bought the building in Jean-Claude's name."

Sebastian released her, as she gasped, rubbing her throat and sucking in air as she glared at him.

Bás walked behind Watchdog, looking over his shoulder at the screen. "Have the police secure Jean-Claude and Patrick. I suspect they're targets as Dominique wouldn't want any witnesses left after tonight. Reaper, you, me, and Bein will go to the apartment. Watchdog, you stay here and keep an eye on Dominique until we get back and can explain this to the authorities."

"What about me? If you think for one second I'm staying here, then you don't fucking know me."

"This is a delicate op with an unstable man. You could get killed."

"I'm fucking going with or without your approval."

"Fine, your funeral. Just don't get any of us killed." Bás glanced at Reaper. "Give the action hero a gun."

Reaper approached and handed him a handgun. "You fuck this up I'll shoot you myself."

"Fair point. Just get her to safety. I don't care what happens to me after that."

Reaper nodded and they headed out the door. He hadn't lied. He didn't care what happened to him after tonight. The only thing he cared about was making Snow safe.

CHAPTER 24

THE ONLY THING KEEPING SNOW FROM PASSING OUT FROM THE PAIN AFTER the second bolt of electricity was shot through her body was knowing her team would come. They'd find her and figure this out. She had to be ready when they did.

"This was the first apartment me and your mother ever shared, you know."

Snow looked up at the man who'd raised her, trying to see something of the man he'd been. He'd been unconventional and difficult, but she'd thought he'd loved her in his own way and perhaps he had but now all she saw when he looked at her was resentment. "Did you love her?"

Henri was watching his phone. "From the day I first laid eyes on her she was like the other half of my soul. Until her, nobody understood me. Not my parents, my friends, nobody until her."

"Sounds perfect."

"It was and then Jean-Claude came along and turned her against me. Convinced her I was unstable, that I wasn't good enough for her." A cruel smile came over his lips. "But he'll get his, him and that bastard son they share."

"You're going to kill them."

"Not me, no. Dominique arranged that part."

Snow's drooping eyes snapped open wide. "What?"

Henri grinned, revealing all the secrets of the clever plan he'd hatched. "I always knew she'd come back to me, and she did. She helped me fake my death and the plan began. We dragged that idiot judge in because we knew it would help us if we were ever caught. An inside man if you will."

"Sebastian is in on it too?"

"No, he has no idea apart from the fake identity. No, Domi and I did this together. She told me about her husband's dirty history and that she had the Caribbean Pink. We planned to kill Jean-Claude and Patrick. Let them take the fall for the attack and bring you back into the family. Dominique would announce our love to the world, and we'd rule France together." His face contorted. "It was going perfectly until I found out she'd betrayed me again."

"When you realised I wasn't your child."

"Exactly, so now I'll take the diamond as planned and Dominique will die along with you and her husband and son in a tragic family suicide."

"How did you find out?"

Henri chuckled. "That idiot husband of hers mentioned a daughter in an email he sent her about Patrick and then it all clicked. You never looked like me, you're nothing to me, but another reminder of her betrayal."

"So, you're going to kill me?"

For the first time since this began, he looked regretful, and Snow wondered if she could still talk her way out of it.

"I have to. It's the only way I can walk away."

"My team will never let you get away with this."

"Maybe not but they won't find me, so it won't matter."

Snow knew that was true. If Henri disappeared, it would take years to find him. He was an expert at living off the grid, they'd done it her whole life.

Silence fell between them, and she moved, trying to get comfortable and thanking God she was double-jointed but still, her muscles burned with pain and fatigue.

"Will you let me down? I won't run."

Henri rose and walked to her, his eyes raking over her in a way that made her skin crawl. He was the man who she'd called daddy and now, because his DNA didn't run through her veins, he was looking at her with lustful eyes.

"You look so much like her at the same age."

His hand skimmed her cheek, and she knew he wasn't seeing her. He was seeing Dominique, the woman he loved and who'd betrayed him again in his eyes. The pair of them were utter sociopaths and sadists. She wondered if he'd killed before and knew from the way he was behaving he probably had.

Had all those people who'd looked too closely at them and suddenly disappeared, really just left or had he killed them to protect what he had? Had she really been raised by a serial killer and not known it?

"How many people have you killed?"

Henri's head snapped back in surprise before he walked away shaking his head before looking back, a smile of pride on his face. "I taught you well, Sabine. I knew you'd figure it out."

"How many?"

"Over the years probably fifteen or so, but I had to keep our secret."

"Our secret. I had no idea. I thought they left me, that I wasn't enough, even for my dog."

"That mutt would've got us caught."

A sound above them made them both look up before a crash sounded just outside the door. Henri wasted no time, rushing to put her between him and the door, a gun held tight to her head. Snow waited, her pulse hammering with adrenaline as the door came smashing in and it was the best sight in the world as her friends rushed inside guns pointed at Henri. She was shocked at the sight of

Sebastian in black fatigues, a gun raised and steady on Henri. Snow stilled at seeing him, her heart breaking at the beauty of the man who'd offered her everything, all for it to be a lie. Yet her traitorous heart didn't care, it galloped away with seeing him there looking like an avenging angel, ready to go to war for her.

Reaper stepped through first, and as he did a click made them all still as Henri laughed.

"You didn't honestly think I'd leave myself without a way out, did you?"

Reaper raised his hand to stop everyone from moving. "It's rigged."

"Enough C4 to raze Paris to the ground."

He must have set it up when she was still out, setting the trap like he always did. He'd known Dominique would betray him, so he'd planned ahead. He was nothing if not a planner.

"If you leave this room, it blows. If you cut her down, it blows. I suggest you evacuate the area as you have exactly five minutes before this building is dust."

With a kiss to her head, Henri inched backwards and like before, slipped through a hidden exit and was gone.

Sebastian went to move inside but Reaper stopped him.

"No, if you come in, you'll be trapped. Help Bás and Bein get everyone out."

Seb moved past Reaper. "Like fuck I will. If she stays, I stay."

"Seb, no. Fleur needs you."

His eyes found hers and she longed to believe the emotion she saw in them. Longed to believe he loved her like she did him, but he'd proved he didn't by lying to her.

"I watched you protect me when armed men shot at you, and I vowed there and then that I wouldn't let that happen again. You're mine, Snow. Mine to love and mine to protect, and if you're here so am I."

With that he stepped over the threshold and came to stand beside her, his strong arms easing around her aching body. Drawing in his scent she sagged against him, knowing she couldn't let him take too much of her weight or it would detonate the bomb.

"You shouldn't be here."

"I couldn't be anywhere else. I love you, Snow."

Her eyes moved away from him as she fought to give into the words he was saying, knowing that they couldn't be true and even if they were, how could she trust him again after everything.

"Excuse me for interrupting this little declaration of love, but I need to see if I can figure out this rigging so we don't all go boom."

Snow nodded at Reaper knowing he was the best at this in the entire team. "Best get to it then."

As Reaper worked moving carefully and quickly, she tried to take her mind off the fact they were minutes away from possible death. "I can't believe he got away."

"He didn't. Dominique knew about the tunnel and warned us before we left. Bishop had just flown in as backup and was waiting for him at the secret exit he thought nobody knew about."

Sebastian's grin warmed her cold body as much as his arms around her did. She knew he was shielding her from sight as much as he could too and was glad of it.

"Got it."

Reaper moved the bed and behind it was the bomb and a mobile phone, a timer ticking down and already leaving them only two minutes to go.

"Talk to me, Seb, distract me."

"Did you know that falling in love has a similar effect on the body as cocaine?"

Snow laughed. "Really?"

"Yep, it's scientifically proven."

"You've been spending too much time with Watchdog."

Seb gave a lopsided grin, which made her heart flip, making her believe every word he said.

"You might be right. I also know that vacuum cleaners were originally horse-drawn."

"You're lying."

"Nope, I wish I was."

Snow sobered as she caught the clock on the timer tick down as Reaper unscrewed the case on the phone.

"We're gonna be okay, Snow, and I'm going to spend the rest of my life showing you how much I love you and proving to you that although I'm not worthy of you, I'll try every single day to make myself better."

Tears pricked her eyes and a sob bubbled in her throat. "I love you, too."

Seb cradled her face in his hands and kissed her tears away. "If this is all we ever have then I consider myself blessed to have known you and had that time."

"Fuck!"

Seb and Snow looked at Reaper.

"What?" They both demanded at the same time.

"It had a back detonator. We have thirty seconds to figure out the code."

"Try Dominique's birthday, the fourth of July nineteen sixty-five."

They watched as Reaper put the code in and the screen flashed. They only had two more attempts.

"Shit."

Snow closed her eyes trying to replay every second of her life with Henri. Her eyes popped open, and she saw the clock had fifteen seconds to go.

"Zero, four, zero, five, one, zero, zero, eight."

Reaper punched in the code and as the clock hit two seconds the light went green.

Her body sagged as Sebastian took her weight and she groaned with the pain that shot from her shoulder joints from hanging for so long.

"Fuck, that was close."

Seb kissed her as he gently unhooked the rope and eased her into his arms, removing his shirt and slipping it over her head. Moving to the door, he carried her up the stairs, a smirking Reaper behind them, covering her back as he and her work family had always done.

Bein and Bás rushed to them as Sebastian gently set her on her feet, keeping his arm around her as he massaged her shoulders.

"Did you get him?"

Bein looked at Bás. "Can you believe she'd even ask us that?"

Bás smirked or at least it was for him and nodded. "Henri Goubert is on his way to jail. Interpol are handling it."

"He killed so many people. All my life he's been killing, and I didn't know."

"You were a child, and an impressionable one, why would you?"

"I should've seen his evil." Snow shivered and Sebastian held her tighter.

"He didn't want you too. Now, let's get you back to base and we can update you on everything we know. Interpol will want to know everything, but we can have Watchdog send them an anonymous packet with all the information. Either way, Henri and Dominique are done, and you can get back to your life."

Snow glanced at Seb knowing they had a lot to talk about and decide on, but for now, she just wanted to hear Fleur's voice and have a hot soak in the bath, before sleeping in her man's arms.

CHAPTER 25

SEBASTIAN NEVER THOUGHT HE'D BE SO PLEASED TO BE IN A BUNKER, BUT this place felt like home to him and after everything that happened in France, he needed to hug his niece. His arm wrapped protectively around Snow, he was glad they'd let him leave the blindfold off for this descent into what was her home.

Bás had explained a lot about Shadow as Snow slept off the last vestiges of her attack and trauma. He knew she'd heal physically, but it was the emotional scars he was concerned about.

For two days all she'd done was sleep, her body cuddled up to him as if burrowing inside. Little did she know she was already so deep in his heart that he'd never be free and for the first time in his life, he didn't want to be.

As the doors swept back his face broke into a wide grin at the sight of Fleur, her entire being humming with excitement. Snow rushed forward, sweeping the child into her arms, and spinning her around as she rained kisses on her face. "I missed you."

"I missed you too, but Val says I can be her 'prentis."

"Wow, an apprentice already? You must be doing so well."

Fleur nodded like a bobblehead, pride in herself evident and making him hope he was at least doing something right.

Seb made his way to them. "Hey, munchkin, you got some of that for me?"

Fleur reached her arms for him, and he took her as she wound her tiny limbs around his neck. "I missed you too, Uncy Seb."

"Good, 'cos we missed you lots and lots like jelly tots."

He leaned down putting her on the ground as she wriggled like a worm. She instantly took Snow's hand and dragged her away. Seb watched them as Snow turned to him with a happy smile, happier than he'd seen her since everything went down.

He felt a presence beside him and turned to see Reaper beside him. The two had forged an unspoken peace since Snow's rescue and them almost dying. Seb knew he didn't have romantic feelings for Snow or vice versa. He loved her like a sister like he had Lucinda, and he was glad Snow had that in her life. God knew her blood family were a fucked-up bunch of dickwads.

"You gonna do right by her?"

He was still a nosey bastard though! "Not that it's any of your business, but as soon as we can get a second to talk, I'm going to ask her to marry me."

Reaper whistled. "Marriage. That's a big commitment. You sure you're ready for it?"

Seb continued to watch as Fleur pulled Snow into the apartment they were sharing there, and his chest tightened with that familiar ache. Ever since the attack, every moment he didn't have eyes on her left him with a sick feeling in his belly. He knew it was some sort of post-traumatic stress. He'd come so close to losing her and now he couldn't bear to be away from her. It was like an obsession, but right from day one, Snow had felt like a powerful force who'd spun into his life and claimed him despite his pathetic attempt to fight it.

"I love her, and I'll do whatever it takes to be with her and keep her happy and safe. I don't know if I'll make a good husband, but I'll spend every day trying to be the man she needs."

Seb tilted his head to Reaper who lifted his chin. "Make sure you do, or it won't just be me who'll hunt you down, it will be the entire team."

"Understood, but it won't happen."

"You tried her cooking yet?"

Seb winced, remembering her attempts at cooking. "I have."

"And you still want to make her your wife? That there's love."

Seb chuckled as Reaper walked away, fingering the ring box in his pocket that had been there since the day before when he'd slipped out to the finest jeweller in Paris and picked it for her.

After a quiet dinner just the two of them, they sat in the living room in front of the couch, Snow cuddled into his chest as he wound strands of her hair around his fingers, loving the silky texture.

"It's good to be back."

Seb kissed her head. "Fleur sure missed you."

"When do you think we should tell her about who I am to her, or do you not want to?"

Seb lifted Snow so she was straddling his lap, her pussy brushing over the hard edge of his erection. "Whenever you're ready to explain it."

Snow rocked her body over his dick, making him groan and grasp her hips to still her motion.

"I don't know where to start explaining."

"Just give her the cliff notes. Tell her that the man who is her father is your brother, but you don't really see each other."

"Yep, that sums it up."

"Do you want to see him or Jean-Claude?"

Snow reached forward, her hands resting on his chest as she played with the buttons of his shirt and his cock tried to punch a hole through his trousers. "Maybe one day but for now I'm just happy for it to be me, you, and Fleur."

Seb's heart kicked up a gear at hearing her say that. "You want us to be together?"

Snow sat back, her walls rising in front of his eyes. "Don't you want that?"

She made to get off his lap and he stilled her, his hands holding her hips in place. "Stop running from me, Snow. I do want that. I want us to be a family and for that to happen, you can't run every time you think I'm saying something else."

Tears filled her eyes, and it almost broke him to see the strongest woman he knew hurting.

"You lied to me, Sebastian."

Sebastian swept away the tears that fell down her perfect cheeks with his knuckles. Guilt eating away at him. "I know I did, baby, and I'm so sorry."

The flood gates open for the first time since she'd been rescued from Henri Goubert. "And I know I lied too, but it was my job, and I was trying to protect Fleur."

"I know."

"I'm sorry I tricked you, Sebastian. I went into this job expecting to hate you, thinking you were like Dominique. Instead, I found a wonderful man who loves his niece and will do anything to protect her."

"Not just her. I love you, Snow. I know I fucked up, but I promise you, I didn't know who Henri was to you until that day at the safe-house in France and I panicked. I was in so deep, and I knew when you found out I'd lose you, and I wasn't ready for that. I won't ever be ready for that."

Snow sniffed, wiping her eyes with the back of her hand. "What are you saying?"

"I love you and I want us to be a proper family. I want you to have my last name, to wake up with my face between your legs every day. To fall asleep knowing how lucky I am to have you in my life. To knock you up and see you round with my baby. I want to marry you."

Her hands covered her face in shock, and he sat up more wondering if he'd fucked it all again by not giving her the romance she deserved. "If you want me to do this with more romance and all our friends watching I can, but please don't say no. I need you in my life, Snow. You're my soulmate, the love of my life, and I can't lose you."

Her hands cupped his cheeks and she laughed through a sob. "Stop. I love you too and I want all that with you."

"Are you saying you'll marry me?"

Snow nodded a grin on her face. "Yes, I'm saying I'll marry you."

Relief sharp and hot flowed through him as he brought his mouth down on hers in a way that sealed everything he felt for this woman without words. She melted into him, her arms snaking around his neck as an urgency consumed them both.

Standing with her in his arms, her legs wrapped around his waist, he prowled to the bedroom. Laying her down on the bed he fell to his knees. Taking the ring box from his pocket, he flicked open the lid.

Snow gasped at the exquisite princess cut diamond nestled in a platinum setting, two smaller diamonds on either side, representing him and Fleur. Seb took the ring and slipped it on her finger knowing it would fit perfectly.

"It's beautiful."

"I know you've probably seen the best jewels in the world, but I thought this fit our family and how we met."

He felt hesitant for a second, butterflies in his belly as he waited for her reaction and he hoped, no, he knew, he'd always feel that with her.

"I love it, it's perfect."

Seb leaned in and kissed her, showing her everything she meant to him and more as he undressed her and made love to her in just the diamond engagement ring she wore.

EPILOGUE

T<small>HE FAMILY-RUN HOTEL ON THE EDGE OF THE</small> M<small>ALVERN</small> H<small>ILLS WAS STRUNG</small> with fairy lights, the room where she was getting ready had its own twinkling Christmas tree lighting up the corner of the room. Snow looked into the mirror and couldn't believe the radiant woman looking back at her.

Her hair was up in loose tendrils, a small tiara held in place on the top of her head with pins. The ivory wedding gown was simple yet suited her and made her feel like a princess in every way. A deep V neckline in satin with spaghetti straps held the low back before sweeping into a huge ballerina ballgown of taffeta.

Nerves tickled her tummy and she found it hard to wipe the smile from her face she was so excited to become Sebastian's wife.

"Will you be my mummy 'ficial now?"

Snow spun in her seat to look at the little girl who'd caused all of this goodness in her life. Fleur had on a pale pink dress with silk flower petals sewn into the net hem, her hair in a sleek bun, and a mini tiara that matched Snow's on her head.

Snow reached for her, and she came closer as Duchess and Lotus looked on. Both women were bridesmaids, as well as Aiofe and

Valentina, who was currently making sure the groomsmen were in place.

Snow had no worries. Her stress from the day before that everything would go perfectly had slid away into a calm rightness. "Yes, I'll be your mummy officially."

She and Seb had talked when after the engagement. Fleur had asked if they could be her mummy and daddy now like the other kids at school and they'd decided to officially adopt her and end the confusion.

Snow knew it would be confusing when they did tell her the details, but for now, she knew her birth mummy had gone to heaven and her aunt and uncle were now her parents. The adoption was a formality, and they'd have the paperwork next week when they came back from their honeymoon. Patrick hadn't contested anything, and as he wasn't on the birth certificate, he didn't have any rights. Lucinda's birth parents were both dead, killed in a car accident shortly after she was born. That was the reason for her adoption and Snow wished she'd known how much they'd wanted her. The couple were newly married and in love from what they could find out.

"I love you, Mummy. You look so pretty. Daddy is going to think you're a princess."

Snow would never get used to those words and knew Seb felt the same. So much had changed for them this last six months, some of it hard, most of it good.

Now they shared their time between London and Longtown. Her role in Shadow had changed in some ways but they'd adapted and having Seb on board as an advisor helped too. He'd retired as a judge, wanting to be able to travel with her and give Fleur the attention he never had from his parents. He looked after the family money now, telling her it meant something as they were building a new generation for it to benefit.

Valentina came rushing in, a smile on her face, the dusky pink of the bridesmaid dress making her look like a model, and perfectly suited her skin tone. In fact, all her friends looked gorgeous.

"You ready to do this?" Snow glanced at Duchess who gave her a smile before she hugged her. "I'm so damn proud of the woman you've become. I'm proud to call you friend and I'll kick his ass if he hurts you."

Handing her the bouquet she stepped back and let Lotus take her place. "Congrats, Snow. You bagged a good one, but he's bagged a priceless gem."

"Thank you, Naz." Lotus only let them get away with calling her by her real name on special occasions, and today was one of those.

As the others hurried out with Fleur chattering happily, Snow knew that, as they approached the new year, it would be filled with love and adventure and more important to her, the family she'd always craved and loved with all her heart.

"You look beautiful."

Bás had been the one she asked to give her away since he was the only man who'd been any kind of father to her in the last five years. The rough brogue of his voice sounded scratchy, and she wondered if today was the day for emotions to overflow.

"Thank you."

He led her down the stairs and she heard the music start as her bridesmaids walked ahead of her. She didn't see the flowers or the faces of her friends, and family of choice, but she knew they were there. The men from Eidolon, with their wives and children. A few of Seb's close friends, and even Margaret's sons who Seb had set up for life with a financial trust that would make anyone's eyes water.

All she saw was the man she loved, dressed in a black tux, his eyes wet as he watched with so much love in his eyes she could hardly breathe. Bás kissed her cheek and handed her over with a whispered warning to bury his body if he hurt her.

"You look like a dream."

His voice wobbled and she had to fight her own tears as the vicar led them through the vows. They'd said their own vows in private, just the two of them, wanting it just to be them when they opened their hearts. Seb had changed but he was still her grumpy, private, hot boss and always would be and she wouldn't change a thing about him.

Then it was done, and Seb was kissing her as if they were the only two people in the world, his kiss promising a lifetime of love and passion.

Pulling back, he looked into her eyes. "Fuck, I love you, Mrs Alexander."

Snow smiled as she glanced at Fleur to make sure she hadn't heard. "I love you too, Mr Alexander."

She thought hearing her new name for the first time would be strange, but it felt right. Like it should always have been this way and maybe that was because he was her soulmate and she'd been made for him as much as he had her.

Later as they danced between the couples, the food served and booze flowing, she wondered how this was her life. "How did I get so lucky?"

"I was the one who got lucky and speaking of lucky, when can we get out of here so I can fuck my wife in that spectacular dress?"

"Seb!" she warned even as her body ached for all he promised.

"What? I've been hard since the second I saw you."

She hadn't missed that fact and had been teasing him mercilessly through dinner, earning her growls and moans under his breath that only she could hear and made her glad this dress was so poufy so nobody could see how wet she was.

"Another hour and we can go."

They were going to stay in the honeymoon suite that night and were flying to Barbados for two weeks, with Fleur staying with Val, her favourite surrogate aunt. She hoped she'd get pregnant while they were there. She wanted a big family and so did Seb and if not, the practice was fun and if practice meant perfect, their child would be the most perfect kid in the world.

Seb kissed her, dipping her back as they danced. She laughed, catching the eye of the man who was her brother in every way but blood. Reaper was dancing with his current charge, Princess Lucía, and if the current sexual tension between them was anything to go by, they were either having wild monkey sex or they were about to. Although he didn't look happy about it and neither did she but when he thought nobody was looking, Snow had seen the way he looked at her with longing and she did the same with him.

Was theirs a case of star-crossed lovers who couldn't be or was it more than that? Snow didn't know but as her new husband led her up the stairs to their room, she didn't care. He was the only thing occupying her mind and body.

"I love you so much, Sabine Alexander."

"You like saying my name now?"

"I do, it feels right. Destined."

As she loosened his tie and ran her hands over his chest making her shiver, when they got to his belt, she smiled. "My husband the romantic."

A growl made her shriek before he lifted her, throwing her on the bed and crawling over her. "I'm not romantic, I'm hot. A fucking sex god, and one who's about to get some payback for all the teasing you did today."

Snow laughed her whole body feeling happy and alive. "You're all those things but also romantic."

"Only for you, my Snow. Only for you."

I hope you enjoyed Sebastian and Snow's story. If you want to read about Reaper and the woman who brings him to his knees, then click on the link below.

Purchase Royal Salvation Now

Not sure? Read on for a sneak peek of Royal Salvation, Reaper and Princess Lucía's story.

SNEAK PEEK

His heart racing, Justice Carson, aka Reaper, ducked his head inside the barren home of one of the elders of the village. For days he and his men had been in search of the leader of the Islamist Extremist Group known as the Islamic Emirate. The leader, Abdul Omar, was meant to be hiding out in the village that was nestled in the Hindu Kush region close to the Salang Tunnel, which linked Northern Afghanistan and the Parwan Provence and was a crucial point of conflict in the war between the groups.

A muffled scream tore through the dirt walls of the deserted home and he raised his weapon. He and his men, of the Australian SAS Charlie Squadron, were leading this mission and as the detonation specialist and bomb expert, it was his job to make sure they didn't find any of the IEDs that were scattered around the mountain like sprinkles on a kid's birthday cake.

Moving through the dark space, the cool of the coming night bit into his skin, even through the thick military-grade clothing he wore, the bergen on his back heavy with supplies.

Seeing nothing, he moved through the village, nodding to his teammate Joker who was across the sand path that separated the village down the centre. This was a six-man team, himself, Joker, Denny, Monk, Chess, and Playboy. The latter was a man he couldn't stand and tolerated for the sake of the team, and because of who his father was.

Playboy was just that, a man who thought he was a gift to women and thought that every female should fall at his feet. He was arrogant, cocky, and a fucking danger to others, but his commanding officer wouldn't hear of it.

He was a good enough soldier, but not good enough for this team. He and everyone else knew it, but he was protected in a way he never should have been, and it would cost someone their life one day.

As Joker and Denny ducked into the home across the way, an eerie feeling of dread worked its way up Reaper's spine. It was something he'd learned to listen to from a young age. As a boy, he and his younger brother had known that if you got that feeling it meant their father a—well-respected Officer in the Australian Military—was in one of his moods.

As the oldest, Reaper had always protected his brother Caleb, who couldn't take the hits he could.

It had made him a man, or that at least that was the mantra his father spouted to justify the abuse he meted out to his oldest son. In some ways that was true because Reaper could just about take any beating he was given and not flinch. It was how he'd got his name. His friends said he was so close to the grim reaper on a few occasions in his career that he was probably him wearing Justice Carson's skin.

The sound came again, a muffled scream but louder than before and he motioned for Monk to go around the other side, and they'd converge on whatever or whoever it might be. The formation of three two-man teams worked well for them, and he knew Playboy and Chess would've cleared the area already, but he couldn't get that feeling out of his head.

As he slid his body along the wall of the hut, he angled his weapon so he wouldn't be caught off guard, a vow he'd made the day he'd stood up to his father and told him if he ever touched either one of them again, he'd put him in the grave. Far from being angry, his father had seemed proud, the crazy fucker believing he'd made him a man.

Rounding the corner, he stopped for a second, not sure what he was seeing until the horrific scene in front of him became clear.

Playboy had his pants around his knees and had a woman, no, a girl of no more than sixteen, pressed against the cold wall of the hut raping her. Chess, who he'd believed to be a good man, was laughing as he made lewd jokes about her as she cried and struggled to get free.

Reaper struggled to understand what was happening. They were looking for a damn terror cell and two of his men were raping a young Afghan girl and laughing about it.

Filled with sudden rage, a red mist falling over everything, he launched himself at Playboy, the shock on his face would have almost been comical if his crime and the disgust Reaper felt hadn't been so visceral.

His fist landed in the other man's face, and he felt the bone crunch underneath his blow. He beat him until his arms gave way and someone pulled him free from the silent man whose screams had died down.

Reaper looked up and saw Joker and Monk detaining Chess. Turning, he saw Denny was the one who'd pulled him from Playboy, who was alive but badly beaten. As far as Reaper was concerned, he was lucky he hadn't killed him but he believed in the justice system and would drag his ass home so he could face charges of rape.

Seeing the wide-eyed look of the girl cowering on the ground, he moved toward her. She shrunk back, terror in her eyes. Reaper held out his hand, only wanting to check she was okay but knowing how frightened she must be amongst these foreign men who'd invaded her peace tonight and attacked her and each other. "It's okay, I just want to make sure you're okay."

Reaper knew she had no idea what he was saying but he hoped

his voice conveyed that he wasn't a threat, when, of course, he was. All of the soldiers there were a threat in some way, whether they wanted to be or not, no matter their intentions.

He tried again asking if she was okay and she nodded. He moved closer, knowing that Joker and Monk had his back. Those were two men he wasn't wrong about. Her startling blue eyes and blonde hair beneath the robes she wore were surprising in this region.

He couldn't help but stare but dragged his eyes away from the child back to Joker. "Find out if anyone in this village knows who she is."

Backing away, he removed a blanket from his bergen and offered it to her, which she took, as her body curled into itself. He could hardly look at her without feeling a blood-boiling rage for the piece of filth who was unconscious on the cool sand. He'd made more work for them by doing what he had. They'd likely have to carry Playboy out of there now. Although a big part of him wanted to leave the animal here to die from his injuries, he knew he wouldn't do that.

When he looked back the girl was gone. He and his men spent an hour looking for her, moving in and out of the properties, avoiding the glances of the women who kept their eyes averted and the men who, although not warriors, looked ready to kill to defend the people from the men, up until that night, they'd been helping.

Gathering their gear, they headed out to the landing zone where they'd exfil and report back to base. The trek was long but uneventful, only made difficult by Playboy who was moaning now in pain.

"Shut the fuck up, you pervert, before I really give you something to cry about."

"Come on, boss, it was just a bit of fun."

Reaper's cool gaze cut to Chess, who was watching him as if he was overreacting on a food order being wrong, not the attack on a young girl.

In the back of the helo, Reaper launched himself across the seat and grabbed Chess by the throat. "Bowling is fun, football is fun. Raping an innocent girl is not fun. It's a crime, you mother fucker."

Chess was turning blue, but Reaper didn't care. He wanted the man to understand but with sudden clarity, he knew he never would. Any man who had to be told that what they'd done was wrong would never see the act for the vile, disgusting thing it was.

Letting him go, he stayed silent on the flight back. Playboy was stretchered away as soon as they hit the ground and he and his team were separated. Sitting in his dirty, filth-ridden clothes, he thought about the girl and prayed to a God he wasn't sure was listening that she'd recover.

His commanding officer ushered him inside the room and closed the door. Twenty-four hours later, his illustrious career with the Australian Special Forces was over. His CO had been sympathetic, but Playboy was the son of a high ranking general and thus protected.

Reaper had thought he'd be prosecuted, that he'd get his just desserts, but he was being sent home to recover before he was returned to the very role that Reaper was being stripped of. His team had come to see him as he packed his gear, the picture of him and his brother the only personal item he had.

They'd told him how Chess had said his words were lies and despite their testimony, the brass had believed Chess and Playboy.

Two weeks later he was in a bar in his hometown of Cairns where his mother was from and still lived since she'd divorced his asshole of a father, nursing a ten-year malt at eleven am in the morning.

Tossing back the fiery liquid he slammed the glass down and motioned for the bartender to bring him another. As he contemplated his life and the screw up it had become, he wondered what he'd do now. Perhaps he could stay with Caleb and his husband John for a while.

They lived on the Gold Coast and were both successful architects with a beachfront home. Caleb had reached out when he'd heard what happened from their mother, but he hadn't been able to face anyone yet.

A presence beside him made him look left to see a man with dark hair and wide shoulders take the seat beside him. Reaper wasn't in the mood for talking. He recognised a fellow operator when he saw one and had no intention of being friendly.

The man ordered a drink and sat quietly sipping the liquid for a good half an hour before Reaper'd had enough. Turning he glanced at him through bleary eyes, and he wondered when the last time he'd been truly sober was. "Do I know you?"

He paused with his drink halfway to his mouth and looked at him. "Nope."

"Then what the hell do you want?"

"I just want to know if you're finished wallowing in self-pity yet or if you need a few more days to pull your head from your ass."

Reaper heard the British accent and frowned before he realised the insult the man had thrown down. Standing, Reaper swayed. He'd obviously drank more than he thought. "What the fuck did you say to me?"

The man ignored him and ordered two coffees from the bartender.

"You don't fucking know me."

"Don't I? Justice Carson aka Reaper. You have a brother Caleb, who is married to John. They're currently trying to adopt a child. Your mum lives a quiet life in Cairns working for a local law firm as a personal assistant. Your dad is Major Malcolm Carson and a complete hardass."

The man stood and he was a smidge taller than Reaper's six foot two inches and slightly broader but also a few years older. A flicker of a memory lingered in his brain but was gone before he could hold on to it.

"Let's get a seat and you can decide if you want to come work for me."

Feeling suddenly sober, Reaper followed the man to a corner seat with a table and took the chair facing the door as the other man angled his chair to do the same. "Who are you?"

"My name is Jack Granger and I run a private security company."

Reaper moved to stand. "Not interested."

"That's fine, but if you walk away, you'll never get your chance to have revenge on Playboy for what happened in the Hindu Kush."

Reaper snarled, his lip curling in open hostility as he grabbed for the man's throat.

As fast as he made contact, he was laid flat on his ass, the other man standing over him with a deadly glare. "You ever lay hands on me again I'll fucking bury you where you stand. Do I make myself clear?"

Still reeling from the quickest takedown he'd ever seen, Reaper got on his feet, a grudging admiration forming in his gut. Rubbing the wrist where Jack had twisted it with such speed and put him on his ass, he sat opposite and watched in silence as their coffee was delivered.

"Everything good here, mates?"

"Yep, all good," Reaper responded, his interest piqued now. What did this stranger know about Playboy and what happened, and why was he there? Taking a sip of the hot brew he felt himself sobering up fast, caffeine and adrenaline would do that to a guy. "How do you know what happened?"

"I told you, I know a lot of things. What I want to know is if you're ready to walk away from this life and begin a new one?"

"Meaning?"

"Fuck, you talk less than I do. I mean, I work for someone who needs good people with a good moral compass who are willing to get their hands dirty to defend those who can't."

"So, a job?"

"No, this isn't a job, it's a life. Your life and existence will be wiped from any database, and you'll cease to exist. Your family will think you work for a mountain rescue company in Wales, but in truth, you'll be doing the jobs the governments are too weak to sanction and saving the very people those governments promise to protect."

"So illegal black ops?"

"Black Ops, yes. Illegal, not exactly. We have the highest authority, but no government or agency knows we exist. You'll sign an agreement, which if broken, won't end with you going to jail. It will end with you in a box six-foot underground."

Reaper should be getting up and walking away but he was intrigued. "Can I think about it?"

"No, when I leave this place so does the offer. You'll wake up tomorrow and have no idea we even spoke."

"How does it benefit me?"

Jack smiled but it held no humour. "Simple, you get revenge on Playboy and Chess. You get to make sure men like him are no longer protected."

Everyone had always thought he'd joined the army because of his dad, and in part that was true. But not because he respected the man everyone thought was a hero but because he hated him and wanted to prove who was better. When he actually began the work though, he'd found helping people and protecting others was something he thrived on.

The night that child was hurt on his watch was the worst of his life, and he'd never forget the look on her face or the feeling of failure inside him. "What happened to the girl they attacked?"

"She was killed by her family later that night. The shame she'd brought to them was too much and they killed her."

Reaper breathed through his nose at the blunt words, his head spinning in a thousand different directions. He'd known it was possible, but he couldn't take her with them, not when two of the six men had been the ones to attack her.

"And Playboy?"

"He's back in the field in your old job as team leader."

"Did the others sell me out?"

Jack shook his head. "No. They fought for you, but Playboy is the son of a powerful man. You were never going to win that fight. But I promise if you join us, you'll get your chance to right this wrong."

"Where do I sign?"

Jack stood, throwing some bills on the table and began to walk away, before stopping and looking back. "Well, are you coming?"

"What? I leave now?"

"You best know those credit cards you have won't work. Justice Carson doesn't exist on paper any longer."

The bright light of the Australian sun hit him in the eyes as they emerged from inside the bar to find a black SUV waiting, the engine running.

"You were that sure I'd agree?"

"Yes."

"How?" His hand rested on the closed door of the vehicle, and he got a good look at the man, recognising Jack Granger as the elite British SAS operator who'd been unceremoniously removed from the Military for unknown reasons.

"You remind me of me."

Reaper arched an eyebrow. "Not sure that's a compliment."

Jack's lips twitched and he had a feeling that was as much as he'd get.

"Pack warm, Wales will freeze your balls off after this heat."

"Can't wait."

"You never know, you might enjoy it."

That was the day Reaper's life took on new meaning and he never looked back.

Order Royal Salvation Now

WANT A FREE SHORT STORY?

Sign up for Maddie's Newsletter using the link below and receive a free copy of the short story, Fortis: Where it all Began.

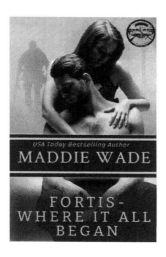

When hard-nosed SAS operator, Zack Cunningham is forced to work a mission with the fiery daughter of the American General, sparks fly. As those heated looks turn into scorching hot stolen kisses, a forbidden love affair begins that neither had expected.

Just as life is looking perfect disaster strikes and Ava Drake is left wondering if she will ever see the man she loves again.

https://dl.bookfunnel.com/cyrjtv3tta

BOOKS BY MADDIE WADE

FORTIS SECURITY

Healing Danger (Dane and Lauren)

Stolen Dreams (Nate and Skye)

Love Divided (Jace and Lucy)

Secret Redemption (Zack and Ava)

Broken Butterfly (Zin and Celeste)

Arctic Fire (Kanan and Roz)

Phoenix Rising (Daniel and Megan)

Nate & Skye Wedding Novella

Digital Desire (Will and Aubrey)

Paradise Ties: A Fortis Wedding Novella (Jace and Lucy & Dane and Lauren)

Wounded Hearts (Drew and Mara)

Scarred Sunrise (Smithy and Lizzie)

Zin and Celeste: A Fortis Family Christmas

Fortis Boxset 1 (Books 1-3)

Fortis Boxset 2 (Books 4-7.5

EIDOLON

Alex

Blake

Reid

Liam

Mitch

Gunner

Waggs

Jack

Lopez

Decker

ALLIANCE AGENCY SERIES (CO-WRITTEN WITH INDIA KELLS)

Deadly Alliance

Knight Watch

Hidden Obsession

Lethal Justice

Innocent Target

Power Play

RYOSHI DELTA (PART OF SUSAN STOKER'S POLICE AND FIRE: OPERATION ALPHA WORLD)

Condor's Vow

Sandstorm's Promise

Hawk's Honor

Omega's Oath

Lyric's Truth (Coming Soon)

SHADOW ELITE

Guarding Salvation

Innocent Salvation

Royal Salvation

TIGHTROPE DUET

Tightrope One

Tightrope Two

ANGELS OF THE TRIAD

01 Sariel

OTHER WORLDS

Keeping Her Secrets *Suspenseful Seduction World* (Samantha A. Cole's World)

Finding English P*olice and Fire: Operation Alpha* (Susan Stoker's world)

About the Author

Contact Me

If stalking an author is your thing and I sure hope it is then here are the links to my social media pages.

If you prefer your stalking to be more intimate, then my group Maddie's Minxes will welcome you with open arms.

General Email: info.maddiewade@gmail.com
Email: maddie@maddiewadeauthor.co.uk
Website: http://www.maddiewadeauthor.co.uk
Facebook page: https://www.facebook.com/maddieuk/
Facebook group: https://www.facebook.com/groups/546325035557882/
Amazon Author page: amazon.com/author/maddiewade
Goodreads: https://www.goodreads.com/author/show/14854265.Maddie_Wade
Bookbub: https://partners.bookbub.com/authors/3711690/edit
Twitter: @mwadeauthor
Pinterest: @maddie_wade
Instagram: Maddie Author

Printed in Great Britain
by Amazon

85261217R00129